BREAK AWAY

Sylvain Hotte

BREAK AWAY
Jessie on my mind

Translated by Casey Roberts

Baraka
Books

Montreal

Originally published as *Aréna 1. Panache*
© 2009 by Les Éditions des Intouchables
Publié avec l'autorisation des Éditions des Intouchables, Montréal, Québec, Canada

Translation Copyright © Baraka Books 2011

Cover by Folio infographie
Illustrations by Pierre Bouchard
Book design by Folio infographie

Library and Archives Canada Catalogue in Publishing

Hotte, Sylvain, 1972-
[Panache. English]
Break away: Jessie on my mind / Sylvian Hotte; Pierre Bouchard, illustrator; Casey Roberts, translator.

Translation of: Panache.
ISBN 978-1-926824-05-5

I. Bouchard, Pierre, 1974- II. Roberts, Casey, 1953- III. Title.
IV. Title: Panache. English.

PS8569.O759P35513 2011   JC843'.54   C2011-900418-6

Legal Deposit, 2nd quarter, 2011

Bibliothèque et Archives nationales du Québec
Library and Archives Canada

Published by Baraka Books of Montreal. 6977, rue Lacroix
Montréal, Québec H4E 2V4
Telephone: 514 808-8504
info@barakabooks.com
www.barakabooks.com

Printed and bound in Quebec

Trade Distribution & Returns
Canada
LitDistCo
1-800-591-6250; orders@litdistco.ca

United States
Independent Publishers Group
1-800-888-4741 (IPG1);
orders@ipgbook.com

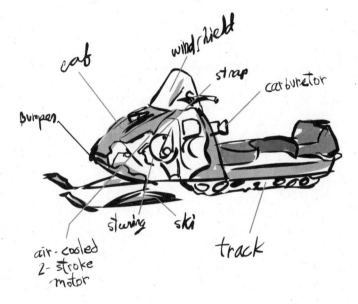

cab

windshield

strap

carburetor

bumper

steering

ski

air-cooled
2-stroke
motor

track

Natashquan

Sept-Îles

Baie-Comeau

Chicoutimi

Québec

Montréal

Chapter One

Yesterday at sunset I drove my quad up to the lake. The day's last light reflected off the water as it rippled under the glacial winds that swept down from the mountain. The fresh air smelled of pine and wet leaves. I stood on the big rock that I use for a summer fishing spot. The fish hadn't been biting this year. I was too nervous, my father said; the fish could smell me.

I held up my two hands to protect my eyes from the sun and confirmed what Tommy had said at practice that morning. We had barely jumped onto the ice when he skated up to me with his stick in one hand, braked to a stop, and lifted his visor. He looked upset, angry even: over the last couple of weeks the Company had gotten right down to the lake, he said.

Tommy was an easygoing kind of guy but he liked to tell tall tales. To hear him talk, they'd turned the area around Lake Matamek into a kind of no man's land. Thankfully it wasn't as bad as I expected, but even then … Tall black spruces once lined the shore to the north; now they were gone. Suddenly, I felt betrayed.

A couple of years ago, Tommy, me, and a few of the other guys turned it into a super spot for hockey. Up in the mountains, the lake stretches east to west, parallel to the river. Strong winds usually sweep away the snow, exposing the clear blue ice underneath as far as you can see.

Except for last year, when we had a bad time with our open-air rink. The first snow in November fell before the lake froze over. Which meant the ice never had time to set and the lake surface was under a couple feet of slush. We shovelled fast and furious, then flooded the surface with snow we had melted up at the cabin and hauled down in metal tubs behind an old skidoo. Hope it freezes up before the first heavy snow this year. If it doesn't, there's no way the guys will be coming up here to play… Especially since they've just built a new arena in town.

Next, I checked out the cabin. One of the porch steps was missing and there were only a few pieces of firewood left. I made a mental note to bring some up and ask my father for the stovepipe brush. Burning spruce clogs the chimney with creosote, which is a serious fire hazard. After ticking off what needed to be done before winter, I climbed back on the quad and took a last look at the lake. When I turned the key in the ignition the motor misfired. For a second I was worried. But soon enough it began to hum like normal and I took off at full speed.

I took the trail up to the Company road. There, I saw just how bad the damage was: they had cut more trees than you could count and hauled them away, leaving debris all over a three hundred metre wide corridor that ran several kilometres up the mountainside and disappeared over the other side. I got off and walked along for awhile; I could see where the big machines had churned their way through the bush and the mud.

It was already dark when I headed back to town, weaving my way through the maze of bush trails. No sweat; I could have found my way even in the worst pea soup fog. Then, to stretch out the ride I turned off on 3rd Side Road. When I reached the pumping station at the end of the road I gunned it, and took off.

By now the lights of the town began to glimmer against the dark water. One hand on the handlebars, I turned up the collar of my plaid jacket to cut the cold and yanked my hat down low over my forehead.

Just then the engine began to cough and backfire. Then died. Worried now, I tried to restart it. The starter cranked but the motor wouldn't catch. I pulled my flashlight out of the luggage compartment and began to check the motor. Needless to say the batteries were shot and the light, which was dim to start with, went out.

I sat there on my quad like some sort of idiot, wondering if somebody would be coming down the road. Maybe once a day somebody did, but it was already getting kind of late. I knew I was in for a long hike. After rolling the Suzuki to the side of the road, I set off at a steady clip, figuring I'd be late for supper.

After about a minute I saw the lights of a house.

The Pinchaults are the kind of poor folk you find in these parts, deep in the backwoods. They live in a run-down old house with a rusty roof, with an old barn leaning off to one side in the back. They've got some chickens and two flea-bitten horses that are so old it's hard to believe they can still walk. There's stuff all over the place, junk of every description scattered here and there.

Their kid Stéphane is a guy my own age, tall and thin, with a huge nose jutting out from his acne-covered face. He's been getting his butt kicked in the schoolyard ever since first grade. But these days, he acts so bizarre that nobody goes near him. The last time somebody got it in mind to mess with him, Stéphane started screaming like he was possessed by demons. He grabbed the guy's throat with two hands and started choking him. It took two teachers to finally pull him off. You can tell the constant bullying he's had to put up with over all these years has affected him. But at least nobody bothered him after that. One thing didn't change. He spends all his time talking to himself and collecting insects and little animals.

I'm not sure why I didn't just go straight on home. I guess one reason was I was cold, but I also felt some kind of morbid curiosity that made me want to see for myself, even though I had goose bumps at the mere thought of setting foot in the strange house that people were always talking about down at the garage and the grocery store. I wasn't afraid of Stéphane. For me, he was nothing more than a weirdo. It was his father, Robert, who scared me, and fascinated me too.

I had heard nothing but bad about him ever since I was little. He was violent and alcoholic, people said. Recently he'd fallen off his horse and broken his hip, they said. The animal had had enough of his drunken rider and sent him flying. The story went that after he recovered from the accident, he beat the horse to death with a steel shovel in a blind rage. It all sounded so low-down and unreal, I just couldn't believe it. What kind of person could be that cruel? But... still... rumours and nasty stories can get to you and there I stood, paralyzed, in the middle of the road, not knowing what to do. Finally, curiosity won out, and I started down the driveway that led to the foreboding Pinchault homestead.

The only front entrance was at the top of the stairs that led to the first-floor balcony, so I made my way to the door at the side of the house, which was lit by a bare bulb hanging precariously by a couple of wires. I shot a glance at the old barn before I started up the steps to the door. Before I could even ring the doorbell the door swung open with a sudden clack. Startled, I jumped back down the stairs, set to take off, picturing Robert Pinchault about to jump on me like a maniac, a steel shovel brandished over his head, about to chop off mine.

But instead, the person who appeared in the doorway was a girl. Her looks took my breath away. She was wearing jeans and a t-shirt. Arms folded over her chest, she shivered; the movement made her long curly hair shimmer ever so slightly. Even though her face was hidden by the shadows, I could see her big eyes looking at me, questioning.

"Hello," she said. "Can I help you?"

She said it like she was greeting someone selling candy bars or bingo cards door-to-door. I didn't answer, lost in the sound of her voice, which could have belonged to an older woman. In fact, she did seem a bit older than me, maybe a year, not more than that. I could tell she was cold and beginning to get impatient. I stood at the bottom of the steps, silent and still.

"Can I help you?" she said again.

"I've broken down."

She motioned for me to come in, and I did, taking the steps two at a time. Then, she closed the door behind her, lightly brushing up against me as she slipped into the kitchen.

"Come on in," she said, standing near a table.

I stepped into the house that I couldn't help thinking about every time I took 3rd Side Road up to Lake Matamek. I wasn't that surprised by what I saw: so this was what it was like when people lived close to the edge. The appliances were old and mismatched. The stove was missing an element; the kitchen table legs were held together with duct tape; the floor was missing a number of tiles; dirty pots and dishes were stacked high on the counter next to the sink.

It was obvious she could see the effect the place had on me; her eyes were tinged with disapproval. The way my gaze lingered on every little thing in that room must have seemed either pretty rude or pretty crude.

"I'd like to use your phone," I said.

But a raspy voice shot back, "We don't have a telephone."

In the adjacent living room, a man was standing in front of an old television set. His grey pants were filthy. He was wearing a brown wool overshirt and green and yellow hand-knit slippers. His face was red under a big, bushy cigarette-stained mustache. It was Robert Pinchault, and it was clear he'd been drinking.

"If it's not the great McKenzie," he said provocatively.

"He's broken down," his daughter curtly responded.

"Your car's broken down?" asked Mr. Pinchault.

"My four-wheeler," I answered. "The engine's dead, it won't start. I'd like to phone my aunt so she can come and get me."

"There's no telephone. I'll take you home."

Pinchault walked with a limp, proof positive that he really had fallen off his horse. He plopped down on a chair and took off his slippers, revealing a pair of old grey socks and toenails sticking through the holes. He laced up his old work boots, which were worn right down to the steel toe, threw on his hunting jacket and tugged a baseball hat down over his bald head. The door slammed behind him as he went out. I didn't move an inch.

"You don't have to go with him if you don't want to," his daughter said to me.

Her skin was pale, with freckles on her nose and cheeks. Her Pinchault nose was large and curved, but where on the men of the family it would be big or even grotesque, on her it was elegant and refined, and gave her beauty a fascinating quality. It was a bold intruder on the face that harboured those pale green eyes.

"My name's Alex," I said, holding out my hand.

She smiled and slid her small hand into mine, which compared with hers was huge and stained with motor oil and spruce gum.

"I'm Jessie," she said.

At that moment, my attention shifted from her eyes to the top of the steps leading to the second floor. I caught sight of two legs with white socks that reached up to a pair of hairy calves. Someone was there, listening to us. Jessie turned, leaned forward and looked up the stairs.

"Stéphane?" she said. "What are you doing up there?"

Without an answer, the hairy legs disappeared up the stairs. I heard the car start up and I headed for the door.

Mr. Pinchault sat waiting for me in his big '70s vintage American car. Remembering what Jessie had said, I was weighing whether or not to walk home. But then I saw her father, who had gone to the trouble of getting dressed so he could drive me home, waving through the cracked windshield. The door hinges creaked and I sat down beside him on a blanket covering the front seat's torn vinyl upholstery.

"It's a '78 Chrysler Newport," he said, lighting up a cigarette, "400 horsepower."

The muffler was shot and there was a god-awful roar every time Robert Pinchault gunned the big engine. Exhaust leaked into the car through the floor and we both had to keep our windows open so we could breathe.

He twisted around and with one arm on the edge of the seat, backed up to the road at full speed.

Turning on to the dirt road, he continued rolling in reverse until he pulled up even with the quad. His cigarette dangling from his mouth, he said, "Nice machine... what is it, orange?"

"Yep."

"What kind is it?"

"A Suzuki 250."

"4 x 4?"

"Yep. 15 speed, diff lock ..."

"Damn," he said.

He threw the car in gear and spun the wheels, kicking up gravel.

I buckled up and settled into my seat, one hand gripping the door handle. Pinchault's cigarette smoke was getting in my eyes, so I leaned my head close to the window so I could breathe the maximum fresh air. As the big Chrysler cruised down 3rd Side Road at full speed in the middle of the night, I could hear the rocks rolling away after hurtling into the rusty floor under my feet. Every time we hit a bump the Newport swayed back and forth a couple of times: the suspension was gone.

A couple of times I turned towards him, but didn't say anything. I could make out the outline of his body in the darkness, his two hands on the steering wheel. The bright orange glow at the end of his cigarette lit up his big nose; the smoke curled up under his mustache.

It must have been about then that I saw the moose on the road. But I can't say for sure because I don't really remember a thing.

◉

I found out about the accident later.

We went off the road into the ditch just before the railroad tracks. Nothing spectacular or really bad; just a run-of-the mill, ordinary crack-up. Except that the old Chrysler's passenger seatbelt was shot and my head smacked into the windshield. And I lost consciousness.

I had a big old bruise on my face, right above my eye. But that wasn't all. The car's underbody, just below my right foot, crunched into a huge rock. My ankle was twisted when the floor gave way. I ended up with a massive sprain.

I came to in a room next to an old man who was coughing to beat the devil. His raspy deep cough pulled me out of a troubling dream probably brought on by the drugs. Slowly I sank to the bottom of a deep dark sea, into an abyss from which I could hear the sound of whales singing. They called to me and I didn't know if I should try to get away or swim closer to them. All of a sudden, their cries changed into a racking cough, the old man's cough. I took a deep breath as if I had just come up from the bottom of the ocean, and with difficulty I opened my swollen eyes.

My eyelids were glued shut and I had to strain to unstick them. Someone was leaning over me, wiping the tears that were running down my cheeks.

"Easy now. This won't take long."

I recognized my aunt Sylvie, my father's sister. Every time she pressed on my eye with a cotton pad to absorb the liquid, the pain was more than I could take. She must have seen me wincing since she kept apologizing.

She was leaning over me with a smile on her face, wearing the same scarf she always wore on her head. She caressed me softly with one hand on my tummy, making circles like when I was little. Ever since I had lost my mother, she had taken care of me as if I was her own kid.

"Hey there," she said. "You know, you're not looking that great."

I guess I must have cracked a bit of a smile. Sylvie asked me how it was going, and I had to clear my throat a few times before I could get out that I was okay. My foot was throbbing like crazy. My first thought was about the hockey season and I asked for my father. She said that Michel had left early that morning to get him at the hunting camp. If the trails weren't too soft after all the rain we'd had, he'd be back later on in the day.

"They're going to keep you under observation until noon," said Sylvie. "The doctor's coming by to look at you. Then, we'll head home. But before that, the police would like to see you."

"How come?"

"To ask you some questions about the accident."

A worried expression came over her face, and I could tell that she too would like to ask me "some questions." I closed my eyes; finally the drugs were starting to take effect. Then I drifted off to sleep, her warm hand still on my stomach.

A nurse woke me up. My aunt had run out to do some errands and would be back to pick me up around noon, she said. A little later I saw the doctor, who asked me how I was feeling and poked me all over, looked in my eyes and ears and examined my ankle. I felt my throat tighten when I saw my swollen foot, red and blue with some yellow spots. The doctor could see I was troubled. I had been lucky not to tear the ligament, he told me; I'd be back on my feet in no time.

When the nurse changed the bandage on my face, I could see the wound above my eye in the mirror. I had really smacked myself. A long cut ran from my hairline to just above my eyebrow. There was definitely going to be a noticeable scar.

"Does it hurt?" she asked.

I shrugged my shoulders, as if to say it was no big deal.

I was slouched down in the waiting room when I sensed someone close by. Suddenly a feminine silhouette had materialized to my side. I shook myself out of the daze I was in to see Jessie standing shyly in front of me. Quick as I could, I pulled myself together and sat up in my chair.

She wore a long blue coat hanging down over jeans tucked inside of calf-hugging boots. Her hair was tied back behind her head and her body swung from left to right like a pendulum. She smiled, forlornly.

I couldn't avoid noticing her subtle fragrance when she sat down next to me.

"My father's having a really hard time," she said with difficulty.

"Is he hurt?"

"No, he's okay. It's just that …"

She went on, looking at the ground.

"… I'm afraid of what might happen."

She'd had a tough life, growing up with her mother in Quebec City. If it wasn't alcohol it was hard drugs, and now her mom was back in a rehab again. Which was why Jessie had made up her mind to come back to the Côte-Nord for a while. It would be better to live with her dad, she figured, than end up in a group home.

I'd lost my mom when I was just a kid, so I could feel a lot of empathy for Jessie when she talked about her past. I managed to blurt out a few comforting words, nothing brilliant, and I promised her that everything was going to work out. Even if I couldn't explain how.

She smiled sweetly at me. I wanted to kiss her and tell her I liked her. But then, all of a sudden, she stood up. She thanked me and said she had to be going. Then awkwardly headed out the door without a backward glance, leaving me wondering what I'd done wrong. But I hadn't even made a move on her. Soon enough, Sylvie showed up with a Dollarama shopping bag in hand. She showed me the tablecloth she had bought to cover the cracked melamine on the kitchen table.

"Who was that?"

"Umm… a girl."

"A girlfriend, eh," she said, winking at me.

From me, nothing.

I'm actually pretty good with crutches. I got down the hospital steps hopping on one foot, then swung myself across the crosswalk in three giant strides. Out in the parking lot, navigating between cars, I could cover a lot of ground. Sylvie was behind me, getting all worked up and hollering at me to be careful.

To be honest, I have to admit I was hurting, plus it wasn't so easy to squeeze into my aunt's little Toyota.

The long drive home from the hospital in Baie-Comeau wasn't my idea of a good time. Not like I was worried about the 138, which we took every day. It's just that Sylvie is a woman who really likes to talk a lot about anything and everything. And if you didn't have some reason, real or imagined, to be somewhere else, you'd be in for hours of listening to her.

And when you got to the point where you couldn't take it anymore, all you could do was quietly slip away, forget the reasons or explanations. Unless you're like my father, who's an expert in faking sleep.

"Has he been asleep for a long time?" Sylvia had asked me, last spring it was. We had just returned from a gathering expedition.

I shrugged, keeping my eyes glued to the TV, fingers crossed hoping she wasn't going to treat me to a discussion of the new mushroom patch she'd uncovered upstream from Lake Whatsits. My father, slumped on the big green couch, was pounding it away while the Canadiens nursed a 2-1 lead over the Bruins eight minutes into the third period. Yeah, right. Even Sylvie had a hard time believing that, rolling her eyes as she went off to bed.

"She's beginning to clue in, I think," I told my father. "I don't think it's working anymore, your little act."

"Did she say anything about it?" he asked.

"Nope."

"I'm telling you, it's still working."

And he pumped his fist. A goal for Subban. Montreal was up, 3-1.

My aunt is a seamstress at a Betty Brite in the mall. She hems workpants and replaces broken zippers. Besides that she runs a gathering business, selling mushrooms and berries to restaurants on the Côte-Nord and in Quebec City. But what sells best are the savory herbs she picks along the shore. The little business was rolling so well that she offered me a job, and so I worked for her all summer. Even if strawberries and raspberries can get a little boring, I must admit that I like picking herbs in September. I take Sylvie behind me on the quad and we head off down the big sandy beach. When she taps me on the shoulder, it means she's found a good spot. We put on our rubber boots and spend the day filling our pails. I love the river; it's like the sea, with the wind and the sound of the waves. Sometimes, when Sylvie moves off in the distance, out of sight and caught up in her work, I lie down on the sand and daydream, looking out over the water. I could watch the clouds fly by for hours, especially when sky and water merge and you can't tell where one ends and the other begins.

Highway 138 rolled by under the wheels of the little car, while my aunt dodged the astronomical number of potholes that pit the pavement. Then we got stuck behind an 18-wheeler loaded with logs. Normally that was all Sylvie needed to get cranked up over the pulp and paper companies that were clear-cutting the forests. She'd go on and on with the same rant she'd been repeating ever since I was old enough to toss in my two cents worth. But, to my surprise, she didn't say much after we left the hospital. Including not a word about the rape of the boreal forest.

I looked at her; she had both hands on the steering wheel and a serious expression on her face.

"What do the police want?" I asked.

"To ask you some questions about the accident."

"What is there to talk about, it was an accident."

"They want to know if Robert Pinchault was drinking."

After the old Chrysler had gone off the road, Mr. Pinchault had hurried over to a neighbour's, Jean St-Pierre, to get help. I was unconscious, and the cut on my forehead was bleeding pretty badly. The two of them carried me to Jean's car. Jean wanted to take Robert Pinchault to the hospital too, but no matter what St-Pierre said, he just wanted to go home.

They made me wait a bit at the police station before directing me to a small office whose occupant was a big chap named Gagnon. He had a round red face and wore a shirt that was too small for him; the buttons over his stomach seemed about to pop. As usually happens in these parts, we already knew each other.

"That's pretty bad luck, with the season just getting underway."

"Yeah," I said, shrugging my shoulders.

"Maxime tells me you're leading the league in scoring."

I shrugged again. What good was it to be the leading scorer if your team loses all its games, I felt like asking him. But I decided to keep my mouth shut. He perched his glasses on the tip of his nose and typed something into his computer.

"Can you remember if Robert Pinchault had been drinking?" he asked.

" No."

"Did he have alcohol on his breath?"

"No."

"When you were at his place … did you see any open beer bottles or anything that would suggest he had been drinking?"

"No."

He frowned, joining his hands on top of his desk.

"What I don't get is that Jean St-Pierre's testimony seems to suggest the exact opposite."

Once again, I shrugged.

"So how did the accident happen?"

"There was a moose on the road."

Chapter Two

No sooner did we get home than I had my head in the fridge and four slices of cheese in my hand, ready to cook up a couple of grilled-cheese sandwiches. I was waiting for the cast iron frying pan to heat up when I heard my father's big red pick-up roll up the driveway and come to a stop on the gravel. Through the kitchen window I could see the cloud of dust. I looked up at the ceiling.

As soon as I heard the truck door slam shut, I knew my sandwiches would have to wait. I turned off the stove and leaned against the counter, hands in my pockets.

The house shook as his heavy hunting boots thudded up the steps. He opened the front door and slammed it shut, yelling at the top of his deep voice:

"ALEX!"

Louis McKenzie is one big dude: six feet four, more than two hundred and fifty pounds. He's a hunter, a guy who loves to eat wild game and he's been working for the logging Company since he was fifteen. Most of the time he's quiet and easy-going, but sometimes he can really blow his stack.

When he saw me in the kitchen, he looked me over sheepishly. Then, with an awkward but touching gesture, he walked over and hugged me. Sure he meant it, but I knew him too well. It wouldn't last.

He took off his orange hat and let his grey-streaked hair tumble down his back. My father is an Innu. A man who's proud of his roots. He's always worn his hair long and likes to tie it with leather strips. When people tried to get under his skin he always maintained his dignity. Not to mention that, six feet four inches and two hundred and fifty pounds can produce a certain level of respect in other people.

He looked at my ankle and I answered his questioning glance.

"It'll be a couple of weeks before I'm back on the ice." He cursed and punched the wall with his big fist. Sylvie yelled out his name from her bedroom, upstairs.

My father has spent all his life in the bush. Born into a desperately poor family, he quit school young and went to work for a logging company when he was fifteen. He got his foot mangled by a machine and after that, he became a foreman for a mill subsidiary that marked trees for cutting. Later on, the Company shut down the subsidiary and hired the guys back as subcontractors. That's one way to cut costs. For my father, who was always hungry for freedom, it was an acceptable solution. Did he really have any choice? There was only one employer in the whole area: the logging Company.

He always dreamed of a better future for me. My natural talent for hockey had always brought him a lot of hope. That's why my ankle injury had kind of morphed into "his" ankle injury, the one that had turned him into a cripple who walked with a limp and made him grimace with pain whenever the weather was damp and grey. That had to be the reason he punched the kitchen wall.

"What in the world were you thinking, going off with that drunkard?"

"He wasn't drunk. It was a moose."

"A moose?"

"There was a bull in the middle of the road and we went in the ditch."

"In the middle of hunting season? The whole North Shore is crawling with hunters. Guns are going off all over the place, and you, you see a moose right on 3rd Side Road?"

"Un-huh."

"For two weeks I'm perched in my hideout, three hundred miles away from here, and you're telling me that all I really have to do is to 'park' right beside the tracks?"

"I guess so."

My father, shaking his head from left to right, went to the fridge and poured himself a tall glass of Pepsi and sat down at the table. He was still steaming, tapping his index finger on the shiny melamine. I could tell it was going to be a while before I'd be able to eat my grilled-cheese sandwiches.

"Mike said that he just left you on the road."

"He didn't just leave me, Papa. He left me with St-Pierre who drove me to the hospital. He wasn't feeling good and just wanted to go home"

"To sober up."

"He wasn't drunk."

"I'm going to go over to Pinchault's, and I'm going to give him a piece of my mind." He smacked the table with his empty glass, got up, and put on his hat. I told him not to do it, that it wasn't worth it, that Robert Pinchault was down and out, nothing more. Mind your own business, he told me.

I followed him outside. Three 45-footers passed by on the 138, one right after the other, the Jake brakes making an earsplitting racket. I grabbed my father's arm to hold him back. We were a sight to see, him with his mangled foot and me with my sprained ankle. He looked at my hand on his arm, and then gave me a withering look. I let go. He told me to get back inside. Leaning on my crutch, I told him right to his face:

"You promised that the Company would never cut the trees up at the lake!"

"What lake? What are you talking about?"

"You know damn well what lake I'm talking about. Your lake. I was up there yesterday. They've cut right down to it. There's no more spruce on the north shore."

"The government decided to sell off the land. There was no choice, we knew it was going to happen."

"And your inheritance? Your beaver traps? Your *natau-assi*... I guess that's no big deal," I added.

And at that, he turned red as a beet; I knew then I'd pushed him too far. I took a couple of steps back onto the porch, ready to escape into the house on my crutches, convinced he was about to give it to me good. But he turned on his heels and climbed into his pickup. Fuming, he spun the wheels in the gravel before squealing onto the highway like a madman, the passing cars honking and jamming on the brakes to make way for him.

Sylvie came to see what was happening. She put her hand on my shoulder. Now it was my turn to fume. I was grinding my jaws like I wanted a mouthful of broken teeth.

"Are you going to be alright?" she asked me.

"He wants to make Pinchault pay... the jerk."

"Look," she said. "You know your father can fly off the handle. He's probably going to stop off at one of his pals', have a beer and calm down. Louis isn't much of a fighter, you know that."

I nodded in agreement.

But Sylvie didn't know what I'd told him about all the clear-cutting, my father's beaver traps and his family inheritance. I had touched something so deep down in his heart, something so painful to do with his heritage and all the contradictions he'd gone through as a foreman for a paper company, that he'd jumped into his pickup and headed up 3rd Side Road to kick the shit out of Robert Pinchault. After he left, I finally ate my grilled-cheese sandwiches and fell asleep on the old green couch. It was dark when I finally woke up. All the lights were out and it was quiet upstairs. I lay there a long time, arms crossed behind my head, looking at the ceiling and listening to the trucks rolling down the high-way and rattling the house. One thing was bothering me: my quad. I dressed warmly and started down the 138 on my crutches.

Cars and trucks whipped by me on the shiny black pavement. The wind was blowing hard off the open water and I had to lean into my crutches to avoid being blown backwards. A few cars stopped; people from the village, and some acquaintances, asked if they could give me a lift. I was just out for a walk, I told them, that was it. I kept on until I reached town and the Rue du Quai. Turning at the red light, I arrived at Michel's.

Mike, my mechanic, is a family friend. He was the first person Sylvie had phoned when I had my accident. And it was Mike who hit the road at three in the morning to go get my father up at his hunting lodge. He's a little strange, a solitary guy who gets along better with engines and bodywork than with people. He's tall and thin, with long blond hair that's turning grey. He always wears a Maple Leafs hat and a vest with a logo from some old heavy metal band like Black Sabbath or Iron Maiden.

When I got to his shop, I saw that all the lights were on, which was no surprise. Mike is the kind of guy who never sleeps. Whether you stop in at six in the morning or at midnight, he's always in his garage working. He lives in a little house set back from the main drag. It's at the back of the yard, behind a children's clothing store and next to a woodworking shop. The house isn't much more than a shed. I think there's just one room on the ground floor and one room upstairs. And as far as I know, he's never there. Just to sleep, and that's it. He even eats out all the time, at Chez Lisette.

I knew my hunch was good when I saw my Suzuki parked in the yard behind the workshop, just up the street from the wharf. The place was jammed full of engines and vehicles of every description. I came up to the fence and Nuliaq started barking as loud as she could. After sniffing my hand, she calmed down enough to be able to stick her nose though the chain link fence and lick me enthusiastically. Nuliaq is a husky, over thirty years old. Whatever she came down with, it had almost completely blinded her.

After a couple of minutes of fooling around with the old husky, I went into Michel's workshop, a big double garage with a 15-foot high ceiling. Tools were piled everywhere you look, on workbenches, lining the walls and lying on the floor too. Jacks, soldering irons, metal benders, everything. You name it, think of a tool, any tool: for sure Mike will find it somewhere in all that mess.

He was lying underneath a formula one style racing skidoo propped up on hydraulic jacks. He slid out on his creeper and waved hello, then got up, grabbed his Leafs hat from the seat of the skidoo and put it on his blond head. He had lost some weight. His face was long and gaunt.

"I knew it was you," he said.

"Why's that?"

"Nuliaq usually won't stop yapping until I come outside."

"How come she's outside?"

"She's shedding," he said, pointing to a clump of fur mixed in with some used motor oil in the corner. "It's gross! It's all over the place. She's gone senile. She'll bark for hours at a tractor tire."

He opened the door; Nuliaq came in and lay down in her corner, imagining she'd better be good and obey if she wanted to stay inside. Poor mutt. How could she know that it was because she would shed a ton of hair twice a year that she ended up in quarantine?

I leaned up against a sawhorse while Michel put away his tools. I couldn't help noticing the new Stihl calendar with Miss October dressed in a pink bathing suit and straddling a tree trunk, holding a big chainsaw.

"Did your father tell you it was me who brought in your quad?"

"No, but I guessed it anyway."

"Know what this is?" he said, tossing me a spark plug.

I didn't answer, tapping the object with the tip of my finger. The electrodes that ignited the gasoline vapour in the cylinder were completely burnt out. The way he was looking at me, I couldn't tell if Mike was going to give me a lecture or burst out laughing. I shrugged my shoulders; he was right. I should have checked the plugs. There was no excuse for not carrying a spare. Besides that, I should never have gone into the bush without a survival kit: first aid, matches, water, blanket and flashlight with fresh batteries. And definitely, spare parts and some tools. Unfortunately, I'll probably never be that disciplined, and Michel will always be giving me that look.

He flicked a switch and the big floodlights that lighted the yard went on. We went outside and found ourselves immediately on the biggest playground you could ever imagine. For a mechanic like Mike, that is.

You could find anything and everything in his junk-yard, as he referred to it. Old cars, boats, motors, tractors, you name it. If you think he likes tinkering with skidoos and motorcycles in his free time, his real baby was sheltered up against the side of the garage: an awesome dune buggy he had been working on forever. He'd gone over it from top to bottom. It was purple with flames painted on both sides. During summer, "The Mike" can be seen rolling at top speed down our beaches that stretch forever.

Besides all the scrap metal stacked on big rusty shelves under a tarp, there were parts for repairing boats: trans-missions, diesel engines, and so on. Michel was a handy-man and a compulsive tinkerer, but he actually made his living repairing fishing boat engines.

On the ground, next to my Suzuki lay a huge bronze propeller.

We both looked at it. The name of the boat that it had previously belonged to, *Marie-Belle*, was engraved on it. It had come into Mike's hands after he had done some work on the boat. The fishing boat's owner, short on cash, had given it to him as payment for his work.

"Is it worth a lot?" I asked.

"You bet. But it needs some work. It's unbalanced. I'm going to try to heat it up and whack it into shape with a hammer. If that doesn't work, too bad. I'll hang it over the door the way some folks hang up moose antlers."

While Mike opened the gate, I hung my crutches on the back of the quad and turned the key. The engine started up like a charm. I turned around at the back of the yard before heading out when my headlight flashed on something strange.

There was a curious machine parked behind Michel's garage. Squeezing out a little gas I rolled forward slowly, then I cut the engine and coasted until the quad came to a stop in the mud, in front of the machine. My headlight, still on, lit up the strange contraption. It looked like a cross between a skidoo and a pickle.

"Not bad, eh?" Mike said proudly, wiping his hands on a rag.

"What is this baby?"

"A 1970 Skiroule SX-440."

"Never heard of it."

"Made in Quebec, at Wickham. A Ski-Doo competitor. A collector's item, hard to find. I had to go all the way to Northern Ontario to find it. A guy from Témiscamingue told me that his father had one that had been sitting out on his land for years."

It must have been there for that long. The metal was rusted through and big swatches of green paint were peeling off all over. The headlight was smashed in. The leather seat was torn and mice had gotten into the foam that had spilled out. Steel rods, bent every which way, stuck out from the vehicle's track, which was cut in half and stuffed with hay. Even though it was dark and I couldn't see very well, I was pretty sure I could make out a bird's nest in the carburetor.

"Gilles Villeneuve raced in one of these."

"One of these?"

"Actually, he used an RTX, not this model. They're not as fast as what's around today, but damn close."

"I don't see myself running around in a rig like that."

"Wait 'til I'm done getting it in shape… You'll be jealous."

I shook his hand, wished him good luck with his project, and left. It felt good to be back on my quad, and the time I had spent with Michel had helped me chase away the blues. I rolled down to the port, looking at a fishing boat. In a few days, it would be heading for dry dock in Sept-Îles for the winter.

It was low tide and I took the boat launch ramp down to the beach. I drove slowly, taking in the salty air. Off to one side was the dark mass of the sea. On the other, the lights to the town. I cranked the gas and cruised down the damp packed sand as far as Brown's Road, and took it back to my place. A fine mist came slanting in, driven by the autumn wind. I was cold and soaking wet, my pant cuffs full of sand and mud. The sock that protected my injured foot was drenched. I parked the quad in the garage and hopped up the stairs to the porch, crutches under my arm. Sylvie was waiting for me at the door, wrapped in her bathrobe.

She heaved a sigh as she went into the house. She didn't say a word, but I'm sure she wanted to tell me that I shouldn't be riding the quad, that I was hurt, but … The only person who could have stopped me was my father, who had gone back to his hunting cabin. I hoped he'd never get him, the moose I mean.

When I got out of the shower, I went in to Sylvie's room and sat down at the foot of her bed. She was wearing her glasses on the tip of her nose, reading a novel. After a minute, she put down her book and looked up at me.

"How come you broke up with Mike?" I said.

"He's not my type."

"But he's a good guy."

"Yeah, but you need to be more than a good guy to get somewhere in life. Me and Michel, it never worked and it never will."

"Never?"

"What am I supposed to do with a guy who's always either fixing a machine, talking about machines or smelling like machines? That's all he knows; that's all he can do. It can get as boring as hell."

"But that's the way he is. That's him."

"Yeah, but there's a limit. He's getting kind of old for that stuff. You know, his dog's named Nuliaq."

"So? That's a nice name."

"Look, that's the Inuit word for 'wife'. So fine, let him stay with his dog. I've got other fish to fry."

I smiled. She asked me why but I didn't feel like saying. She grabbed the pillow from behind her head and hit me with it. I left the room laughing while Sylvie, on all fours on the bed, kept asking me what was so funny. I closed the door just in the nick of time. The pillow she tossed at me hit it instead.

I can't figure out why they're not together. But I've got to admit I get a kick out of seeing my aunt come unglued every time I bring up Michel.

I love the sound of skates on the ice, slap shots, the puck ricocheting off the boards. I swung slowly on my crutches down the corridor the players take to get to the ice. I moved as quietly as I could, as if I were in a museum or a library. As if I didn't want anyone to hear me or to even know I was there.

It was seven in the morning. I swung my crutches along the rubber mat that protected the players' skates. Just as I thought I was in the clear, I heard a door open behind me.

"McKenzie!" called a voice that I knew only too well. It was my coach, Larry. His real name is Laurent. But everybody calls him Larry. He's a decent guy, but we don't hit it off, him and me. For one thing, he's too loud. And for another, he must have bionic ears, 'cause every time I walk past his office, he hears me. I thought he would have been out on the ice with my teammates.

"*Salut*," I said, feigning innocence.

"What happened to our big 'star'?"

"I had an accident. You know that."

"That's what I heard. But I would have rather you called me and told me yourself. I'm your coach, Alex, and I've got a right to know. I've got a workout to plan. We have a game tomorrow night."

One thing I've known since I was a kid is how it works around here: in less than twelve hours, everybody knows what you were up to the day before; who you were with, what you did, why. There was no doubt in my mind that Larry knew what had happened to me. It wouldn't even have surprised me if he brought up the grilled-cheese sandwiches.

"Sorry," I said.

"We're a team, McKenzie. Are you aware of that? We live together and we die together. When a soldier falls in battle, the commander has to know so he can reorganize his troops. Otherwise everyone's going down, down to defeat. You're not on your own, McKenzie. Get it?"

I nodded without saying anything. I never have anything to say to Larry. He's pretty uptight, and the fact that I'm the team's best player drives him wild. A long time ago, he was the best player on his team. He was a local star who played in Major Junior hockey with the Cataractes of Shawinigan. He was drafted 228th in I don't know what year. Then he did a couple of training camps with the Philadelphia Flyers before crashing and burning in the American League, unable to make the big leagues. Regional disappointment.

He joined the Army and became a blue beret in Bosnia-Herzegovina. But he came back completely off the wall. He went into coaching with big dreams for the future. But he never became anything more than an uptight guy whose idea of coaching was to push his players to the limit to get them to perform. The problem with me is that he knows that I don't really give much of a damn. Every time he jaws at me in the locker room and I shrug my shoulders, I get the feeling that he's going to pick up a stick and break it over my head. But I'm his best player, so he can't do it. But whenever he gets a chance to take me down a few notches, like at the present moment, he'll jump at the chance.

He especially likes to give the impression that he has cracked the secret of my success: luck. He gets all worked up at the thought of it. In my own humble opinion I'm no better than anyone else. I'm an average skater. I've got an average slap shot, a pretty good wrist shot. What they say about me is that I'm always in the right place at the right time, that my stick's where it should be, that even my prayer shots end up buried in the back of the net, that opposing defencemen put their turnovers right on my stick, sending me off on breakaways that bring the crowd to its feet. Which is surely what Larry will say one day, when to his delight he can tell everybody what a rotten no-show I really am. Him, he'd known it all along; he'd never gone for the head fake. And that soon, any day now, it would all turn bad for me, like it did for him, back when.

"Hey, McKenzie!" he said. "I'm talking to you. Where's your head at, anyway?"

I shrugged my shoulders and I swear I could see smoke coming out of his ears. He went back into his office slamming the door behind him.

I slid slowly along the boards on my crutches, trying not to slip on the cement floor, when a puck ricocheted violently off the glass above my head. The impact was deafening. I just about had a heart attack. I dropped a crutch and, awkwardly hopping on one leg, leaned over to pick it up. When I raised my head, I saw Tommy and the others: Samuel, J.-F. and Félix, goofing off, walking with their hockey sticks as if they were cripples. I flipped them my middle finger and they started skating in my direction ready to shoot more pucks at me. Just then a shrill whistle blast echoed through the arena. It was Larry, making his entrance. He started chewing my friends out, which really cracked me up. After giving them a mouthful, he started skating like crazy, circling the ice dipsy-doodling just to show everyone who was the best. After his little song and dance, he made the team work up a sweat, doing stop-and-go's.

I sat in the stands and watched them work out, glad I wasn't out there, and daydreaming about riding my quad into the bush up the trail to Flat Top Mountain. There's a sweet little river up there and a path that'll get you to the top if you use the spruce growing in the rocks as handgrips. From high up, the view of the St. Lawrence is awesome. Autumn is great. It's cool and there're no bugs. The birch are all yellow and orange. I love it. It'd be cool if they made hockey players get in shape by climbing mountains.

A blast from the whistle pulled me back to the present. Larry stood at centre ice, surrounded by the team. You could tell the guys were beat. He started talking loudly, his voice audible anywhere in the building.

"Okay guys, listen up. McKenzie won't be suiting up for a while. But that doesn't change a thing. If we stick to the plan, we'll win our share of games."

Finally it happened. Just what I was most afraid of. And why I'd been so hard on my father. At school, Jessie wouldn't speak to me. She was so embarrassed she wouldn't even look me in the eye. But to tell the truth, it was me who was dying of shame.

It turned out that my father never actually hit Mr. Pinchault, but he gave him hell in front of his own children, who had to watch their father break down in tears and apologize. What a mess! Totally off the wall.

I left the arena as soon as practice was over, not stopping to say goodbye to the guys in the locker room. I knew that Larry was ticked off at me and that he would get back in my face the next time he saw me. But I was really hoping to get to school early, just in case she might already be there. The kids that take the bus often get there early, sometimes as much as half an hour before school starts. At the risk of seeming like someone who didn't care about his team, I snuck out the emergency exit. I started up the quad, turning the key slowly as if that would make the engine run more quietly, then took the path behind the arena that led to the school.

I went in the main entrance, waved to the secretary in her glass cubicle, and headed towards the cafeteria. The rubber tip of my crutches squeaked on the linoleum like fresh cheese. When I got there I gave a quick look around. Two people I barely knew came over to me to see how the injury was doing and when I'd be back on the ice. What a bummer, they said; I was their favourite player. But I wasn't exactly what you would call friendly, barely looking at them, eyes darting to and fro in search of Jessie, who was nowhere to be found. I was worried that people might think badly about her family. That they might blame her and her brother, Stéphane. I argued as hard as I could that it was nobody's fault, there had been a moose on the road.

I had barely taken two steps when two guys on the basketball team came up to me giving me high fives. I repeated my story once again, carefully choosing each word, telling how Robert Pinchault had been super friendly and how it had been a stupid accident.

"So why did your father go to bust him in the chops?" asked the six-foot-four blond-haired guy with the thick glasses.

"Maybe you'd like me to bust you in the chops?" I answered back.

They started backpedalling, hands held out, making like it was nothing, calming me down. But I was already over it. Some girls were laughing behind me. I headed over to them and finally spotted her, sitting in a corner of the café, studying with the boys and girls in Sauvé's gang. I started to walk in circles on my crutches, not sure what I should do.

Jonathan Sauvé is a tall junior who's into gangsta rap. He wears long baggy pants and a baseball hat turned backwards. Despite a certain awkwardness, he's smart, calm, collected, and softspoken. But he's a dealer and has the reputation of flying off the handle and getting involved in some pretty uncool things. In a word, a small time boss man.

I wasn't up to facing up to the whole gang just so I could talk with Jessie. There I stood, with all these considerations running through my head, not moving, looking at them, for just a tick too long. I must have looked like a real idiot with my crutches, and my foot all wrapped up in a sock. Suddenly, they all stopped talking and laughing among themselves to look at me in wonderment; everyone except her that is; she'd turned away and was staring at the wall.

Jonathan Sauvé, acting in his capacity as leader of the gang, questioned me with his eyes. Then, making one of his a bit-too-laid-back hip-hop moves, said to me:

"Hey, hockey man. Why don't you come sit with us?"

... as if he was inviting me to go to church with his family.

I turned him down. From the way Jessie reacted, I could tell she was hurting over her father's humiliation. I swung my weight onto my crutches and left without saying a word, head down, realizing that any effort to approach her, the person who had occupied my every waking thought since the moment I had met her, would probably accomplish nothing or make things worse.

That day, I got tossed out of class for talking back to the teacher. The principal sent me to the library, where I was to stay until school was out. A little before 3:30 he came to ask me what was going on. I started to defend myself by saying that the teacher had been looking for trouble, but it was useless trying to talk about it and my rudeness was inexcusable in any case. He said that I shouldn't worry, that what I was going through was tough, that my ankle would heal quicker than I thought. Intrigued as much as discouraged, I wondered as he left the library: Is that all anybody cares about is hockey?

The rest of the week, I stayed in the yard slap-shooting rubber balls, tennis balls, practice pucks—anything I could find—at targets hung on the net, like I wanted to destroy them. Aunt Sylvie came out to tell me that it was 10 o'clock and I should call it a night and hit the sack. But I was like a man possessed, shooting and shooting by the light of the streetlight. Friday, at dinner-time, my father came back from hunting. He hadn't killed his bull moose this year and should have been in a bad mood. But seeing me practice like that, with such intensity, made him happy and he smiled. He came over to me and said hello. I shrugged, not saying anything, and I made a move like in the Kovalev video, juggling the puck on my blade and flicking it up to the back of my neck while leaning forward. I let it roll down my back and turned, ready to strike before it hit the ground. My father broke out laughing, shaking his head from left to right as if he didn't believe it. He reached out to tousle my hair, but I sidestepped him, shooting a couple of balls at the targets on the goal.

As he went up the stairs, I shot a puck that thwacked against the metal wall of the garage. Louis turned to look at me for a long moment without a word. His look was more interrogative than severe. I looked down. He went in the house while I kept juggling pucks on my stick.

I was tired. But I couldn't sleep. I hadn't been able to get Jessie off my mind all week. I had to find a way to see her alone to explain how everything had been a terrible mistake: the car accident, my father's anger, everything. There had to be some way to make sense out of it all. I was sure of it. And I was determined beyond measure to find that way, up to and including making myself look ridiculous.

My ankle had completely healed after a couple of weeks, to my great pleasure, and to the surprise of my doctor who hadn't believed it would mend so quickly. He cautioned me to hold off a bit all the same. But I felt good. So good that I started skating a week before he gave me the go-ahead. My father and Sylvie were against it. They said it was a bad idea; I should wait, otherwise there was a danger of making it worse.

"At your age, you've got to be cautious with an injury like that," said my aunt, probing my ankle. "You're still growing. Imagine if you had to sit out a whole year..."

"That could mess up your career," my father went on, playing the role of the wise old man.

But none of it stuck. With both of them on my case, I felt like I never wanted to play hockey again. But that's a crock. Skating's in my blood. That same morning I had secretly taken the quad, hiding my skates in the luggage compartment. When school was over, I was planning to go to the arena and work out by myself.

The new arena's ice is fast, wicked fast. It seemed like I could go end to end twice as fast when I was in full flight. They had torn down the old arena to build this one. In the old building that dated back to the '60s—my father was three years old—the ice was too soft on account of the obsolete cooling system. The pucks slid sluggishly and passes were always a bit off. And the carooms off the boards were so unpredictable and sometimes so ridiculous that it had turned into a standing joke in the league; visiting teams treated us like a bunch of losers. It had become a real embarrassment for the municipality and one of the main issues in the last elections. The townspeople might argue bitterly when it came to the governments they're supposed to elect, the ideas they're supposed to come up with and the money they're supposed to spend, but when it came to the arena, everyone was on board.

I skated for fifteen minutes circling first one way then the other, getting pumped up by the effort. As I repeated the exercise, the rhythm of my skates became so natural that I was able to do a couple of laps around the rink with my eyes closed, knowing exactly where I had to turn and how much strength I should put into each stroke.

I was shooting pucks at the net from the red line when I saw a light go on in the hallway leading to the locker room. I wasn't supposed to be there and I felt a bit uneasy. Of course, the person headed towards me was the last person in the world I wanted to see: Larry, my coach. But there he was, dressed in his customary light blue jogging suit, baseball hat on his head. I couldn't see his face, just the blue tinted glasses that reflected the arena's overhead lights.

"You've started skating, McKenzie?" he said.

"Yes," I answered, gliding up to him on my good ankle.

"Is your ankle still sore?"

"No. I'm being careful."

"When did you start skating?"

I shrugged my shoulders…

"When did you start?" he repeated. He still had his hat on, and didn't look too classy with his two hands tucked into the front pockets of his coat. He had just come in from outside and was cold. His glasses were fogged. I don't even know how he could see me.

"On Monday," I answered. "But I'm going to take it easy and watch out that I don't reinjure myself."

"And it's already Thursday and it never crossed your mind that we should talk? Don't you think your coach should be informed when his star player gets back on the ice?"

"Yes…"

"Just like you were too busy to show up for team practice last week. You think you can do whatever you want, whenever you want, without thinking about anyone else, is that it?"

"No…"

"I'm gonna tell you something, McKenzie, I've seen guys coming up in my day, guys like you; underachievers that grew up faster than the others and could do what they wanted on the ice. Some of them, a few, have made it to the Major Junior League. But not one has made it to the NHL. Do you know why?"

"No…"

"Heart, McKenzie. They don't have heart. So far, they had it easy. But when it comes time to give it everything they've got, leave it all on the ice, show that they're a notch above the others, they can't cut it. They get creamed. They lose face; they lose the war, their personal war. And then what happens, do you know what?"

Then, I swear, I almost said that those are the guys that become coaches in minor hockey… but I kept it to myself. I was afraid of getting him even more ticked off. The whole time he was jawing at me his face was grimacing and his upper lip was quivering.

"You know what happens to them?" he repeated.

"No," I said.

"They work in a factory or sell insurance door-to-door. And not a day goes by when they don't regret not having done what they had to when they had to do it. Do you get what I'm saying?"

"Uh…. I guess."

He looked me up and down through his no-longer fogged up glasses. Hat still atop his head, Larry calmed down slowly, no doubt proud to have said his piece, and put me in my place. He turned away and walked nonchalantly down the corridor to his office. Maybe he was hoping I was going to thank him the next time I scored a goal.

For a week now I'd been skating every day, getting ready to rejoin the team. I hadn't missed one day practicing shooting in our yard. I could have told him that. Told him that's what I love doing and that that was enough reason. That his G.I. Joe lectures were one big waste of time. But I kept quiet. It was none of his business, it was nobody's business. Except mine. And besides, what could I have said? That since I got injured, the team had lost all five games and had been shut out twice?

I took my skates off and left.

I don't know why I keep doing it. Actually, I do know, and it's completely nuts, but I do it anyway. On a regular basis, during my three-week convalescence, I went by the Pinchaults' on 3rd Side Road, I mean like, plenty of times. Up and down the dirt road I went, pretending I was just doing what I always did, watching out of the corner of my eye to see if Jessie was somewhere on the porch, in the fields, or what I was really hoping for, walking along the road.

She would have decided to go for a walk after dinner, by herself. Just when I would have been passing by. I would have stopped to say hello, and she would have smiled like she used to do. We would have talked a bit, then she would have asked me what I was doing there, and I would have explained that I was coming back from getting the cabin ready for winter. She would have said that she'd like to see it and I would have invited her to climb on behind me. Up at the cabin, she would have gone down to the lake to watch the sunset over the mountain. I would have watched her for a minute, walking towards the shimmering water, the bottom of her jeans caked with mud, her colourful scarf wrapped around her neck and her long curly hair rippling down her back, before going inside to throw a couple of logs in the stove. Then she would have been standing at the bottom of the stairs, asking me if that was the same quad that had broken down before. I would have said yes, a little embarrassed, not really understanding what she was getting at. She would have said that she hoped that it wasn't going to happen again, with a conspiratorial glance. I would have come close to her…

OK, that's pretty over the top.

I never saw Jessie walking along the road. Didn't see a soul any of the six times I went by her place. Unless you count Stéphane Pinchault, who I saw twice down in the field next to the house in the middle of all the trash that was lying around.

If there was one thing that did get through to me from Larry's useless little speech, it was that time was my own worst enemy and that the longer I waited, the more I risked missing my chance. I had to go to the net. I had to talk with her. So, fed—or more like stuffed—by the obsession that made me want to see her so badly, I jumped on the quad and cruised down 3rd Side Road.

I accelerated past the railroad tracks, gulping in the fresh air that smelled like the forest. The day was drawing to a close and the sun shone with a dull gleam that said winter was on its way. The birches and spruce bent down to pay their respects. In the distance, the Pinchaults' unkempt homestead began to emerge through the trees. As I got closer, I was able to make out the car that was parked behind Robert Pinchault's. It was big Sauvé's chopped and lowered Honda.

Sitting on the quad's seat, one hand on the handlebar half-heartedly feeding it some gas, I could see Jonathan Sauvé getting into his car. He looked up and saw me. I raised myself off the seat, tucked my chin into my hunting jacket and blew by the house, looking off in the other direction.

I headed home with the definite impression I was the all-time king of the losers. As I rolled along I could see the streetlights coming on as night fell, forming the royal passage for the king of the jerks; unable to grasp why everything was slipping away from me like sand through my fingers, only the harder I tried to tighten them the faster the sand flowed.

I was really dragging my ass when I came in the house. I hung my jacket on a hook and smelled something that gave me a warm feeling inside. Sylvie was cooking dinner. I plunked down on the green couch and watched some guy yakking away on television. I couldn't understand a thing he said. He was even more idiotic than me, and that made me feel a bit better.

I was about to turn in when I heard the oven door open with its distinctive creak. I got up to go to the kitchen, sliding my feet into my slippers. There was Sylvie, her scarf on her head, holding a huge casserole of shepherd's pie. She winked at me, licking her lips, and asked me to put some ketchup on the table.

"Look. I put some paprika on to redden up the top. Not bad, eh?"

I nodded and sat down, a bottle of ketchup in my hand. My problems seemed to fade to nothing in front of a big thwack of shepherd's pie.

We had each started in on a big serving when we heard my father return from work. He came in, thumping his feet, and slowly stripped off his outdoor clothing while we ate silently. He muttered a few incomprehensible words at the television and then came to join us in the kitchen. He was limping more than usual. You could tell his foot was hurting him. He had spent the whole day in the bush where it was wet and cold. In autumn, his injury always acted up.

He grabbed a beer from the fridge, got a plate from the cupboard, and sat down across from us without a word. Sylvie and I watched as he took a huge swig of beer and then plopped a scoop of pie onto his plate. He drenched it with an unbelievable quantity of ketchup, so that you couldn't see anything else, unless it was a couple of pieces of corn floating in a big red puddle.

"You really can't stand shepherd's pie, can you?" asked Sylvie, teasingly.

He shrugged his shoulders. And right at that moment, he reminded me of myself when I don't feel like answering. I was just about to mention it to him, but he looked so beat that I decided not to and went on eating in silence.

"How's it going?" asked his sister.

"Hard day," he answered, his mouth full.

"Your foot's hurting you?"

"Yeah. And I'm heading out next week to do some marking, up above the reservoir."

"That's not exactly close by."

"A twelve-hour drive."

"That's a long way to go to cut some trees."

"You could say that."

"Is that what's got your back up?"

"Not really. This afternoon, the guys were talking about the mill closing again."

It wasn't the first time that the mill closing down had been discussed, both in town and around our table. Two years back, my father had been laid off for almost five months. And then, no sooner had the mill reopened, and no sooner had new machinery been purchased with government money, than they were back to talking about closing the mill. I'll never figure it out; Aunt Sylvie has. But she keeps her mouth shut around my father, who would just accuse her of being a tree-hugger.

Whenever they start talking about closing the mill, there's this unbelievable malaise that hangs over every house in town. People get anxious. When the mill was shut down two years ago, some mighty unpleasant things went down. Crime went up, and certain things happened that were so bad you can't even speak about them. Guys who people looked up to turned into full-time alcoholics. Popular girls left for Quebec City or Montreal.

My father works as a subcontractor for the Company. He marks trees for cutting. All his tools belong to him. He owns his big new truck. And if there aren't any more contracts or money even to pay for a beer…

"It's going to work out," said Sylvie, the eternal optimist.

"Maybe I should start picking mushrooms with you," said my father.

"Why not? I made two hundred dollars the other day picking chanterelles." She went to put the kettle on for tea while my father grumbled that you can't pick chanterelles all year round. She was in the midst of explaining that a well-organized person, gathering wild berries and mushrooms from April to October, could live comfortably and just take the whole winter off, when she suddenly stopped and grabbed a big brown package that was on top of the fridge. She brought it to the table.

"I almost forgot. The book you ordered on eBay came in."

I pushed away my empty plate and started opening it.

"I'm warning you," Sylvie said to me, "you wanted your present ahead of time, but there's not going to be anything else at Christmas, understand?"

"Yeah, okay."

"What is it?" asked my father, intrigued, leaning over toward me and trying to see. I showed it to him. It was a gigantic encyclopedia that I had found on the Internet. Three hundred thirty pages. More than five hundred colour photos, with rare species found even here in Quebec. It was *the* reference on the subject. There wasn't anything better.

"Since when are you into insects?" he asked.

Chapter Three

Saturday came at last and there I was, perched in the stands, waiting. The arena clock showed one; the game would be starting in a half-hour. I pretty much had the place to myself. I'd come a bit early so I could hang out with the team in the locker room. The guys were glad to see me without crutches, "ready for battle" as Larry put it.

Felix, who's my centre on the first line—I line up on the right, but I shoot from the left—seemed genuinely happy to see me and it felt good to shake his hand. He started giving me the business, asking me if I needed help getting across the blue line. Felix is on the small side and he skates like a bullet. Not weighing much, he goes down easily. For which Larry reads him the riot act: if he doesn't beef up his adductors bad things are going to happen during games; he might as well kiss the National Hockey League goodbye.

Our second-line center is Tommy, my best friend. We love playing together because we complement each other's strengths. We pass the puck back and forth and we have a blast on the power play. Both of us are big and we don't hesitate to use the occasional elbow to clear the front of the net. That's the kind of thing that really bugs Larry. No having fun without permission from him. The first thing he did at the beginning of training camp was to split us up. Tommy tried to argue, but Larry shut him up, saying he knew us well enough, he'd seen us play together before and it wasn't going to happen this year.

"Nobody said it was going to be easy, guys," Larry said. It was the same old pep talk: dig deep down, stay within yourself, you've got to have heart and all the rest.

No worry about losing my seat; nobody was there yet, so off I went in search of three hotdogs with mustard and relish to gobble before the opening face-off. Larry is after me to eat more veggies. I'm getting fat he says, and fat won't cut it in the NHL. You know, honestly, that guy, I'm really starting to hate him.

I gulped the hotdogs down in a couple of mouthfuls and chased them with a big swig of Pepsi. The crowd was streaming into the new arena. A lot of people who knew me came up to say hello. How was I doing? they asked; when would I be back in action?

"Next game, Tuesday night."

"You must be going nuts," they said.

"Yeah, I can't wait."

"Same for us."

It was a long Saturday afternoon.

We got our butts thoroughly kicked, 5-1. At the beginning of the second period, Felix brought the crowd to its feet, getting in all alone and going five-hole for a wicked goal. But that was it. Otherwise, the team was in full retreat. The offence was anemic, the defence back on its heels. Especially Simard, who was catching hell from a couple of rowdies who if you ask me were being really stupid. He's a regular guy, Simard. He gives it everything he's got each and every shift. But he's slow, and it's not a good thing how easily he gets beat to the outside. I saw his family in the stands. His poor mom had to sit there and take it while a couple of drunks called her son every name in the book. Finally, it got so bad that two girls stood up and told the rednecks to zip it. But the horse was already out of the barn as they say. Which is probably the reason why it took awhile before somebody stood up for him. If Eric Simard doesn't pick up his game a notch, his skates are going to get heavier and heavier, and at our level, you can't get away with that for long.

It was glumsville in the locker room after the game. Some of the guys discreetly acknowledged my presence with a nod. A couple of others were jawing at each other in the showers. Which is one thing you don't want to do around Larry because all hell is likely to break loose. And then everyone involved is likely to find themselves skating laps until 6 o'clock. "The team—the soldiers—make up one unit, which has to stick together," as our drill sergeant/coach was apt to say. To give you an idea of how bad things were, Larry didn't even come around after the game to see the players.

I went up to Felix, who was sitting by himself in front of his locker, not speaking to anybody. He already had his coat on and was lacing his boots.

"Your line played alright," I said. "You just caught some bad luck. It could've gone the other way."

"Bad luck?" he said, getting up and slinging his duffel bag over his shoulder. "If that's what you call missing three wide-open nets. Stank up the place, more like it."

We left the dressing room together. I asked him if he wanted to come up to the cabin, but he said no.

○

Outside, you could almost smell the snow in the air. Overhead, the clouds rushing by looked like giant rollers piled one on top of the other. The wind whipped the leaves across the arena parking lot. I asked Tommy if he still wanted to go up to the cabin with me. We could light a fire. I'd stocked the cooler and figured we'd cook ourselves some burgers. But he just shrugged and looked away.

"No, I'm hooking up with Karine at the restaurant."

I had no comeback. He wanted to be with his girlfriend. What could I say? That we'd have fun, just us guys, grilling meat patties and telling stupid jokes? As if. Nothing beats passing time with a girl at a restaurant, hoping to touch hands or bump knees under the table and, if you should be so lucky, a little serious necking later parked on the side of the road.

"Are you going to come?" he asked me.

"I don't think so," I answered. "I'm going up to the cabin."

"By yourself?"

"Yeah."

"Take a break, Alex, forget the cabin. You can always go some other time. It's Saturday night. We're grabbing a bite at the restaurant and then we're going to the Centre to chill."

"It's not my favorite thing, hanging out at the Centre."

All the kids go there to listen to music and play billiards. Tonight, there'll be a DJ. For sure, some people will be dancing. Everybody doing their thing. And me, I'd be just moping around, not knowing what to do, hands in my pockets. There's something about the forest. The more people are around me, the more I hear the woods calling.

"Chloé's gonna be there," he said.

"So?"

"Uh, Chloé…"

"What?"

"Pfff… Go on, go up to the cabin, eat your old burgers."

I got on my quad, Tommy jumped on behind me. He was screwing around. He opened the cooler and asked me how were the hamburgers. I threw it in gear and popped a wheelie. He just about fell off, and gave me an ear-full.

Chez Lisette is a favorite stop for truckers working up and down the Côte-Nord. Folks from around here like to go there to drink coffee and shoot the breeze. There's a section of booths beside the windows. That's where we like to eat and fool around until the waitress finally asks us to leave, seeing as how we're not ordering any more. We like to push it until Gaëtan, Lisette's big boyfriend, gets up from his stool at the end of the counter with his humungous beer belly hanging out of his tee shirt. Gross! Without a word he looks over at us; everybody knows that's it—time to clear out.

I stopped in front of the door to the restaurant. The bright blinking yellow sign that advertised the daily special—fish and chips—lit up our faces. Through the window, I could see Karine and her friends. I spotted Chloé too, with her round face and dark black hair.

Karine, all excited, pointed us out to her friends. But I turned to look at Tommy.

"So, come on," he said.

"Sorry, I don't feel like it. I'm going up to the cabin."

"You know, Alex," he added as he went up the restaurant steps, "maybe you should just forget about Jessie Pinchault."

I practically had to pick myself up off the ground. I wasn't expecting that. Who had I even mentioned it to? Nobody. Not a soul. Why was he saying it, like that? As if it was so obvious. Like he had already thought it through before he brought it up.

"What the hell are you talking about?" I said.

"Everyone knows you're sweet on her. You should hear Sauvé cracking jokes about it."

Sauvé was a jerk, I said, then threw the quad in gear and angled off behind the restaurant to grab the mill road. My first thought was to take 3rd Side Road to act out my stupid little ritual in front of Robert Pinchault's house, but I dropped the idea. Instead, I took the high trail that goes up to the lake. Any way you cut it, 3rd Side Road was out of my way. Everyone knew it's a detour. And now everyone knew I'm sweet on Jessie and that I'm the biggest fool in the whole world.

◉

It was almost dark when I got up to Lake Matamek. I shut off the engine and sat totally still as night fell. The wind blew softly through the branches of the trees, swaying them to and fro. I walked down to the shore. The water was black and little waves, pushed by the breeze, lapped up against the pebbles at my feet. The dark mirror of the lake reflected the thick, wintery clouds. A long shiver ran up my spine and I went inside.

The cabin is a one-room affair with a sleeping loft that has an old moth-eaten double mattress. There's a rocking chair, too, and a picnic table with a bench on each side. And you can't miss the black cast-iron stove— way too big for the cabin—that an old woman who Tommy's mother knew gave us. We couldn't really say no. But the thing is huge and incredibly heavy. You should have seen us trying to slide it on skis up to the cabin in the middle of winter. It's so big it could heat a whole house. A handful of coals can warm up the space in no time and even at thirty below you have to open the cabin door to let in some cold air.

Once the fire was going, I lit some candles and placed them around the room, then looked at the package of ground meat from the grocery store sitting on the table wrapped in brown paper. Next to it, in a flat Tupperware container, was some spread Sylvie had made for me out of ketchup and mayonnaise. I'd been looking forward to this night and I'd hoped all the guys would be here. But nobody had come. Tommy was with his new girlfriend. Félix and Samuel were playing NHL 2011 on their Xbox.

I couldn't be bothered to cook the meat so I toasted two hamburger buns instead, and spread yellow mustard all over them.

The fire was crackling and I told myself I'd better stop feeding it if I wanted it to go out before it was time to go home. But, as if I didn't really want to leave, I opened the stove door and added a huge birch log that immediately burst into flames.

There I was, sitting in the rocking chair, feet propped up on a bench. It was hot as hell inside the cabin and I tore off my boots and coat. I went on rocking as the sweat poured off me. Shadows danced on the particle-board walls, flickering to the rhythm of the candlelight. Outside, the wind whistled in the stovepipe. Letting go of everything in spite of myself, I fell asleep.

When I opened my eyes, it was dark and very cold. The candles had burnt down to their stubs and the fire had gone out in the stove. I didn't know how many hours I'd been asleep. It all seemed unreal. But there was no denying that it was night outside and I was chilled to the bone.

I got up, shivering. It was all I could do to put on my boots my arms and legs were shaking so hard. I put on my coat and threw an old grey wool blanket over my head. I stirred the embers in the stove and added a log, blowing to get the fire started. My brain seemed numb, and I felt like a cave man, the way my thinking was slow and my ideas were confused. Twice, I tried saying something out loud, but all that came out were a couple of incomprehensible gurgles. I hopped to and fro in a squat watching the flames mount higher and higher as the pieces of bark I had slipped under the logs caught.

Just then I heard a noise from outside and froze. The fire was crackling. But I could hear something else in the background, a strange continuous breathy sound. At first I thought the noise was coming from the chimney. But all at once it snapped into focus and became louder. I could hear it clearly now, a long inhale followed by a short and powerful exhale. My heart was beating fast and strong in my chest. The blanket still over my head, I edged to the door and opened it very slowly.

The first thing that struck me was the pale blue morning sky. Dawn was breaking and the wind that had been blowing all night had completely died down; all I could hear was that breathy sound that seemed so close. Something was moving in the lake. Through the trees I saw with amazement a dark mass gliding along the shore. It walked rapidly up to the big boulder and climbed ashore with astonishing agility. Then, seeing me on the cabin's porch, it came to a dead stop and stared me right in the eye.

I had seen plenty of moose before, while rambling through the woods or riding in the car with Louis and Sylvie on the 138. The big *cervidae* were quick to disappear into the bush. I had also seen and touched the bucks that my father and his friends brought back from hunting. But never in all my life had I seen one at such close range, alive. It seemed supernatural. Like a fantasy creature from another world: a gigantic moose with huge antlers.

The sight of the moose staring me in the face brought me back to the night of the accident. It was as if I could hear Robert Pinchault's big car and see the road lit up by its headlights. I remembered the railway crossing sign.

And then, Pinchault's scream and the huge animal emerging from the dark, right in front of us, forcing us off the road and into the ditch.

The animal and I looked at each other for a long moment as if each of us expected something from the other. Our breath merged to form a cloud of morning mist around both of our heads. Before I knew it and without warning he lunged forward, almost touching me. Then, he crashed off into the woods and disappeared among the trees. The air was filled with his smell. I dropped my blanket and hit the ground running after him.

I raced through the trees, my head thrown slightly back, chest thrust out, and body tilted forward, as though my weight alone was enough to keep me running. In spite of my strange posture, I dodged between the birches and the spruces with remarkable ease following the animal's tracks. I ran like a wild man, a madman, without a thought in my mind, no longer able to see or hear the moose, but following a kind of imaginary trail that I couldn't perceive, known only to him, but that I discovered as I went along. He was going around Lake Matamek in a westerly direction, which I had always thought impossible.

In my headlong rush I came to a small bay where tall reeds were growing. Here, the water flows out of the lake and I could see the remains of a beaver dam, covered by grass and bushes, and a few ancient stumps.

I stopped, gasping for breath, hands on my knees. Day had broken and I tried to catch sight of the moose. I ventured out onto the dam so that I could see farther away to the other side of the bay, in the direction of the inlet that had become a large peat bog.

I could clearly see his tracks in the huge mossy carpet, with puddles of water oozing to the surface wherever he had stepped. There he stood, motionless, beside a pile of rotting wood at the edge of the forest showing me his back with his head turned toward me. From as far away as I was, I could still see him looking at me, as if waiting.

I jumped off the dam and sank knee deep into the bog. Even though I could barely manage to extricate my feet from the muck I began walking towards the animal, sinking with every step into the dense mat of grass, mud and murky black water.

It was rough going. My boots were full of water, coated with mud and slime, and getting heavier by the minute. In the middle of the bog I sank in up to my thighs; it was all I could do to pull myself free. Exhausted, filthy, and soaked to the bone, I realized that the moose had disappeared.

I stood there, mouth agape, for the longest time, looking in every direction, trying to find the easiest way back to solid ground. A light snow had begun to fall and three black birds swooped low over my head from a tall pine.

◉

Sylvie was in the garage cleaning up. She had definitely heard me, but didn't turn around to greet me. She was in a bad mood, I could tell. I stepped into the doorway and stopped, motionless for a moment.

"Hi," I said.

"Hi," she replied.

The garage was in an unbelievable mess, as usual. I'd never seen my aunt tidying up my tools before. She kept tripping over the skis of my father's snowmobile, a Polaris 500 he'd totalled last spring when he went off the trail and hit a tree head-on. The engine was completely shot and had to be replaced. Even with all of Michel's know-how and skill, you could tell it was going to cost an arm and a leg. And if my dad does lose all his contracts with the mill, he's not going to be able to get the work done. How was I going to get up to the lake this winter without a snowmobile, I wondered.

"Damn machine!" said Sylvie, tossing a handful of dirty rags onto the workbench. "When is this piece of crap going to the junkyard?"

"You'll have to ask Louis."

"Speaking of which, Louis wants to talk to you. He's waiting for you up at the house."

"He's waiting for you up at the house." The way she said it, I knew I was in for a rough ride. I hesitated for a moment, and thought about hopping back on the quad, popping a wheelie, and making straight for the woods to look for my moose. But sooner or later I was going to have to face him. The longer I put it off, the angrier he was sure to get. Better get it over with right away. Besides, he had heard me pull up. He was waiting for me; that much was clear. And I was right. No sooner had I stepped inside than I saw him standing in front of me.

"Look at you! Where have you been?" he said, giving me the once over.

He was wearing jeans and a light blue shirt. His greying hair hung loose over his shoulders. Me, I was filthy, dripping slime all over the front hall carpet.

"I fell asleep at the cabin."

"How come you're so dirty?"

"I followed a bull moose into the bush this morning."

"You know what, my good man? The way you talk, I'm starting to think I'd have better luck hunting moose in the woods out back, instead of trying my luck at the other end of the world!"

"I'm not kidding," I said.

"And me, I'd like to know when you decide to spend the night up at the cabin."

I sighed: this was an argument I was never going to win. No matter what I said, it was going to be my fault. I flashed back to Sylvie, cleaning up the garage. She must have been up all night, worried sick and, to calm down, she'd started tidying up my stuff.

I know that she loves me a lot and I hate to hurt her.

I thought my father was finished, but I was caught up short when he unexpectedly began throwing accusations.

71

"Alex, if you're going to start getting smashed with your pals, you better hang up your skates right now."

I looked up; couldn't believe my ears. He wasn't making any sense.

"You got me perfectly well, son. If you want to drink, you're coming off the team. Understand? I'm not spending my money if that's how serious you are."

"I wasn't drinking!"

"Just get a look at you, Alex. I was your age once. I know what it's like. I know how things happen. You start off drinking a couple of beers with your buddies and before long you lose interest in everything. Obviously school, definitely sports."

"But P'pa…"

Trying to find the right words, I explained how I'd gone up to the cabin alone, how none of my friends had wanted to go with me, how he could call Tommy's mom and ask her, how I'd lit the stove and fallen asleep. And how when I woke up this morning, there'd been a moose right outside the door and I had followed it up to the beaver dam. And the whole time I was talking I could see the moose running deeper and deeper into the forest, between the dark black spruce branches, before vanishing.

My father heaved a sigh and looked me up and down. He had his hands in his pockets, his shoulders slouched. I recalled seeing him like this before, as if it was all too much for him. He told me to wash up and change my clothes, that it was Sunday and he was making pancakes for breakfast.

When I went up the stairs, he stuck his face in between the stair risers to add a final word:

"You know, Alexandre, you're my son and I trust you completely. I always will, no matter what. I just want us to understand each other and I thought this was a good time to set things straight… And you can stay at the cabin whenever you want."

I went upstairs to take a shower.

The hot water flowing over my head felt really good after a morning of shivering. I leaned over, supported by both hands on the yellow ceramic tile, and let the water run down my neck and back. Normally, I wouldn't have let something like this get to me. But right now, I had a big knot in my throat and there was still that damn fistful of sand that was disappearing like the water swirling down the drain.

Monday morning when I got to school, I took a table close to the cafeteria entrance next to the big wall covered with a hippy-style mural of suns and flowers, where all the school's "rejects" sit during lunch and recess. It was the first time I ever sat there since I began high school. Not because I had anything against those boys and girls. It was just that it wasn't my spot. To tell the truth, I was afraid I might be rejected by everybody else, as if the way they were and the way they acted was catching, like an incurable illness you should avoid at all costs.

But this morning, that's where I was sitting, at one of the taboo tables, and I began thumbing through my new encyclopedia while I drank a carton of milk and munched a granola bar.

From the corner of my eye I could tell that people were checking me out. But I didn't look up. I didn't want to meet their questioning glances, I didn't want to know who was making fun of me, wondering if I'd lost my marbles. Anyway, I knew that they'd be buzzing about it in class and in the hallways. Even the outcasts whose territory I'd invaded—Emmanuel Léveillé, Léopold Durand Jr. and the three Carrier sisters—poorly dressed boys and girls with glasses as thick as the bottom of a bottle, were trying to figure out what I was doing there.

Through the big, mesh-covered cafeteria windows, I saw the rural school bus pull up and the students pile out. I started reading a fantasy novel I'd already read once, while leaving the encyclopedia wide open in front of me to a page showing a giant wasp laying her eggs on a dying spider. The larvae would grow, bit by bit, feeding on the spider, before becoming wasps that would lay their eggs in another spider that would soon be dying in terrible pain. It was disgusting and I knew it would be effective.

I heard the kids come down the stairs, then peel off in different directions to join their friends where they usually found them, in the specific places that they hung out in every day, their spots, like tribal territory that feels good to come home to. A place that felt safe in the overwhelming cacophony that was high school.

Even with my nose in my book, I could sense some people walking towards me. Two passed in front of my table, then a third. A fourth person hesitantly stopped close by, swaying undecidedly. I held still, leaning over my book (which I wasn't reading), pretending to be completely absorbed in it, waiting for my prey to react.

He went for it, sitting down across from me, casting his shadow under the fluorescent lights.

I wondered how long Stéphane Pinchault could have stayed there like that, motionless, without a word. After what seemed to me like an eternity, I raised my head and looked at him.

It was the first time I had seen him up close. I had never approached him and I actually turned away each time we passed each other in the corridors. As I studied his face, I was surprised to see how, well, how ugly he was. What was beautiful about Jessie—her nose, her delicate mouth, her big almond eyes—seemed like defects on Stéphane Pinchault's face. Not because he was scary or deformed. It was more the way he carried himself. The way he moved and his grimacing expressions seemed to be exaggerated expressions of what was going on in his head. It wasn't revolting; it was disturbing. But what was particularly unsettling was the way his eyes, with their large black pupils, flitting and evasive, could sometimes settle on your own. It was as if something was missing somewhere in his mind that would have made him a complete human being.

"Hi," I said.

" Hi," he replied with his raspy voice. He was tall and gangly with pimples all over his big red nose and a sparse mustache of fat black whiskers.

He stood there a long moment, silently looking at me, uncomfortable. I slid the book a little closer to him and I saw him checking it out, glancing at it nervously.

"Go on," I said, "Check it out."

"Can I sit down?"

"Sure," I said, "have a seat, Stéphane. That would be cool."

Okay, maybe I was going a bit too far. A low blow. I saw him hesitate, and look from side to side to see if anybody was watching. I bet everybody was watching, and trying to figure out what the two of us could be talking about. Any way you looked at it, Stéphane Pinchault was the reject of all rejects. He occupied the bottom of the school pecking order. What did he have to lose? He grimaced at me, which I interpreted as his way of smiling. He sat down in front of me and started thumbing through the encyclopedia.

So, what they said about him was true: he was just wild about bugs. He seemed to forget I was even there as he feverishly flipped through the pages, devouring the text. I could see his eyes scanning at top speed from one line to the next. Every time he saw something familiar or pleasing, his face would twist into a grotesque expression and he would make bizarre gestures. He was more like an animal; and I began to ease my chair backward, troubled.

The bell rang; time for class. I had to get going to make my French class in time. Stéphane's a senior, same as me. He's a little bit older, but he's been held back twice. We don't have any classes together. I get pretty good grades but he's in a special education group.

I told him he could borrow the book if he wanted to look through it. He could give it back to me at 3:30, at the end of the day. He nodded vigorously and then melted into the crowd of students, the encyclopedia under his arm.

How could you not feel pity and even sympathy for someone as troubled as him? I don't have an answer for that. I was happy to be able to do something that made him feel good and I told myself that it would be easy going from here on.

It had been a long day at school and I couldn't wait until it was over. I had a practice that night, and the next day I would be playing in my first game since the injury, against a team from the Saguenay with a couple of big tanks on defence. We were playing at home, and I was looking forward to my return in front of the home crowd. It would be fun—the other team's porous defence meant there'd be a lot of ice. I'd be free to skate around, just waiting for Felix to find me with one of his pinpoint passes and thwack!—the puck would be at the back of the net.

Sitting on my quad at the end of the day, I waited for Stéphane Pinchault while the snow that had begun in the early afternoon kept falling. Tommy and Sam asked me what I was doing. They were going to the restaurant, but I told them I'd rather go home. They had just headed off when I saw Stéphane leave the school and head rapidly towards the bus. I stood up to be sure he could see me, but he just kept walking with a determined look on is face. I guessed he wasn't going to notice me. So I jumped onto the sidewalk, ran up to him and stopped him in front of the bus door.

"Hey, Stéphane, what about my book?"

He turned, looking extremely nervous. I repeated what I had said, and asked him how he had liked the book.

Without answering, he reached into his backpack and awkwardly thrust it toward me. Before I could grab it, it fell to the ground. I bent over to pick it up and thumbed through it quickly as I stood up. What I discovered really troubled me. I raised my eyes toward Stéphane; he was looking green around the gills, as if he was about to vomit.

My whole incredible insect encyclopedia, the one that had cost my aunt more than a hundred dollars, was filled with drawings, with meaningless words and lines of zeros and ones. I couldn't believe it. He must have been at it all day without a break. You could even make out latitudes and longitudes like the ones on the maps we studied in my orientation classes.

"They're secret codes," he stammered.

My mouth hanging open, I couldn't get a single word out. Finally, I handed him the book.

"Well… here," I said, "keep it. It's a gift."

He snatched it out of my hands and climbed into the bus.

I backed up a couple of steps while the driver closed the door and started the engine. The big yellow bus, which was headed for 3rd Side Road, passed in front of me. Through the dirty window, I could see Jessie looking at me, sitting in the last seat. The bus headed towards the road and Jessie turned around, still looking at me.

I walked over to my quad with my hands in my pockets, cranked it and pulled my tuque down over my ears. It was snowing harder now; you could see big snowflakes twirling under the streetlights that had just come on. I wondered if this might not be my last ride.

Ready to take off, I glanced in the mirror and saw a metallic blue car coming towards me, Jonathan Sauvé's Honda Civic. He had three guys from his gang with him. They sped right by me, windows down, music blasting. They didn't even give me a look, never even turned their heads, but they brushed by so closely that I had to lift my leg to keep it from getting ripped right off.

I was tempted to give their car a kick and yell insults at them. They're older than me but they don't scare me. I could have defended myself. But what kept running through my mind was Jessie, and the way she looked at me with her big mysterious eyes.

Chapter Four

Larry's pre-game pep-talk electrified us. He was in top shape, bursting with enthusiasm. Up and down the locker room he marched, clapping his hands, exhorting us to outdo ourselves and score some goals. We had to hold our ground, not give an inch, wait for our openings and then surge through like the barbarian hordes of Genghis Khan. The guys were pumped; fist bumping and nodding their heads in agreement whenever the coach boomed out the end of a sentence like a cannon shot.

All his fervour might have seemed out of place. After all, we'd dropped six consecutive games, enough to sap any team's morale. But there was a new ingredient in the mix. And even if Larry would never admit it, it had to do with the fact that I was sitting on the bench in front of locker number eight, dressed to play, back from the injury that had sidelined me. I was quiet and focused. I felt as hungry as a wolf who hadn't eaten in three weeks. I wanted this victory and I was ready to chew up and spit out anybody who stood in my way.

The bleachers were packed to the rafters; the crowd was buzzing. When we took to the ice, some of the fans started yelling my name. A shiver run up my spine; I felt a bit nervous to be carrying the responsibility everyone had put on my shoulders: Larry and his determination to win, my teammates' enthusiasm, and now the fans who had anointed me the saviour who would single-handedly pull the team out of the doldrums. I gingerly tested my ankle, wondering if it could handle game pressure. But a couple of laps in that circus atmosphere convinced me that I was more than ready. The only thing I was still waiting for was the opening faceoff.

I lined up to Félix's right, shoulder to shoulder with the opposing winger, while the official checked that everyone was in position before dropping the puck.

"How's the foot?" asked the guy from Saguenay in front of me.

"You'll find out," I replied.

Félix, quick as the devil, won the faceoff. The guy in front of me lowered his shoulder and threw me off balance for a second with a solid hit, but I was ready for it and with several quick cross steps to my left, hit my stride. I lifted my head just in time to take the pass from our defenceman Vigneault at centre ice.

I spun around and deked the smartass winger out of his shorts. Then, with a quick glance, I saw Félix hit the blue line on my left. He took my pass in full flight. One of the huge defencemen from the other team came up to check him, but missed and went heavy into the boards.

I streaked up the ice into enemy territory. Félix spotted me from deep in the zone. He zipped me a perfect pass and I one-timed it, giving it all my weight: a wicked bullet that just cleared the goalie's blocker.

Score! Top shelf! The crowd went nuts. They screamed as if we had just won the finals. I looked up at the scoreboard clock: twenty seconds. Wow! I skated the length of my bench to high five the guys who were pounding the boards with their sticks.

Larry shook his head from left to right as though he couldn't believe it. And I was happy to have stuck one in his craw.

The rest of the game was a little more ordinary.

We came from behind to win it at the very end after trailing 3-1 for two periods, with third-period goals by Tommy and Félix, and the winner by me with less than two minutes left on the clock. Anthony fired one from the point and I deflected the puck without ever really seeing it. I admit, it was luck. But we won, 4 to 3.

The crowd, afraid we were about to drop another one, erupted with joy, practically raising the roof off of the arena. The guys all rushed over to me, winners for the first time in seven games. Happy, I searched for my father and Sylvie in the crowd. That's when I saw, towering over everyone by at least a foot, Stéphane Pinchault. But the best part—Jessie was standing next to him cheering like crazy. Our eyes met, I'm sure of it. And for one moment, I swear that time stood still. The game, the crowd, the ice, the losing side—all had disappeared. There was nothing but that moment, and the most intense feeling I had ever known.

◉

They were partying so hard in the locker room you couldn't hear a word.

The team was in great spirits; victory had been a long time coming. They went crazy, whip snapping each other with towels and splashing Gatorade all over each other.

But when the coach came in, everything quieted down. No question that despite the win, it hadn't been pretty. They all knew it. Most of all, they all knew Larry wouldn't hesitate to drive it home. But surprisingly he kept it short, contrary to his usual practice of never being satisfied, no matter the outcome. He congratulated us for the "great game," more like a recreation director at an old folks' home. Then, along the same lines, he added that he was happy we hadn't quit and that we had shown enough character to get back into the game and go on to win.

He finished up by saying, "McKenzie, stop by my office before you leave."

After showering and dressing, I went up to Félix to thank him for his wicked assist to start off the game. He told me someone had to be there on the other side of his passes, and that he was happy I was back. We shook hands promising to bust a few heads over the rest of the season, and I headed for Larry's office.

He opened the door and waved me in, dressed as always in his pale blue phys ed director's warm-up suit. I observed him for a moment with his balding head and his blue tinted shades. I never thought the guy was what you'd call 'with it.' But looking at him now, he seemed even more ridiculous. I mean, who do you know that wants to come off like that? Nobody.

When did anyone ever wake up saying: "I think I'll dress like that, I feel like being laughed at." Never. Anyway, one thing's for sure, I can spot him a mile away in the grocery store, so whenever I see him coming with his shopping cart I duck into another aisle. That's Larry. Not a bad coach, people say in town.

We both sat down. It was a tiny office; a little hole in the wall built out of beige cement bricks. Not much to inspire you in this particular coach's office, unless you count a faded old poster of Chris Nilan to let you know who Larry looked up to when he was my age. Supposedly, in his third year in the AHL, Larry took on all comers in trying to make his mark as an enforcer, one strategy for getting to the NHL. But he wasn't the biggest guy and he took more than his share of sucker punches. "Crazy Larry" was the moniker that stuck.

His desk was a mess of paper filled with statistics and hockey magazines in French and English. Perched atop the pile was a gold-framed picture of a young girl, maybe seven or eight.

"That's my daughter," said Larry, who noticed me checking out the photo.

He rotated it towards me so I could get a good look. She had a big smile and red hair like her dad, even if nowadays Larry's hair looks more like faded rust. No doubt it was red when he was younger.

"Mélissa," he said. "I haven't seen her for eight years."

"Where does she live?"

"Last I knew, she lived with her mom in Montreal. I've had to be patient over the last few years; I'm trying to get a court order to be able to see her."

"Why can't you see her?"

"It's complicated," he said, turning the photo so that it faced him again. "It's not easy, a soldier's life, McKenzie."

He looked at her for another moment and then put the frame away in one of the desk drawers. Leaning his elbows on his desk, he looked at me in silence.

"Nice game," he said, lowering his sunglasses to reveal his small grey piercing eyes.

"Thanks," I said.

"Two goals, one assist. Nice comeback after a serious injury. I'm happy for you."

"Yeah, not bad," I said, a sarcastic smile frozen on my face.

"You know that we're not going far if we play like we did tonight."

"I guess."

"They're nice, the magic tricks, McKenzie, the fancy plays, the razzle-dazzle, but if you give the puck away and we're always forced to play in our own end, if you don't get back and defend, if you ..."

"But we pulled it out, Larry."

"I don't give a damn if we won! That's not what I'm here to talk about. It's about you, your game."

Normally, his lectures made me fidgety and I'd stare at the floor waiting for him to finish. But this time, I held my head up, grinning from ear to ear. My mind was a million light years away from Larry's office. I didn't care about the game. Didn't care about his advice or anything else. There was one indelible image planted in my brain: Jessie jumping up and down and cheering her heart out after I had scored the winning goal. Unreal.

"Look, Alex," said Larry, with an increasing tone of confidence, "the team won 4 to 3. You were a factor in three of the goals and your plus/minus is zero. Which means that each time they scored, you were on the ice."

"I know how to read a plus/minus."

"First off, that just looks awful. You can't seriously think you're going to make it to the NHL …"

"Larry, I could care less about the NHL."

I don't know why I said that. Really, I have no idea. I don't think it's even true.

But I said it anyway. And Larry, in front of me, completely froze. He dropped his arms and sank into his chair.

"Okay, if that's the way it is, piss off. There's no point in saying anything more."

I got up and went out.

Slinging my duffel bag over my shoulder, I saw my father and my aunt waiting near the arena exit. I went up to them.

"Bravo," said Sylvie, hugging me and giving me a peck on the cheek. "I'm really proud of you."

"What did the coach want?" asked my father.

"He wanted to congratulate me for a great game."

We drove Sylvie home; she had to turn in early in order to be ready for a day of work at Betty Brite. Some hunters had stopped in the day before and left her a pile of clothes to mend. As usual, my father wanted to eat at Chez Lisette. Sometimes, he seems to get hungry more often than me, even though I'm the one skating.

"I don't want to go to Chez Lisette," I said.

"No? Where do you want to go?"

I knew that Tommy'd be there with a bunch of girls, and I didn't want to run into them. In fact, I didn't want to see anybody. If I could have tossed my father out of the pick-up and ditched him, I'd have done it. I'd have headed for 3rd Side Road. And all the Pinchaults would have welcomed me with open arms.

We would have talked about the game, and then Stéphane and his father would have gone to bed and Jessie and I would have been left alone on the couch to watch television ...

"How about a hot dog down at the dock," I said to my father.

"At this time of night?" he said, surprised. "In October?"

"Yeah."

"It's kind of windy down there. And cold."

You can't be serious! If I'd have invited him to eat a salad, he wouldn't have said a thing, and we would have been at Chez Lisette in no time. But, seeing as he was a big fan of hot dogs with mustard and sauerkraut, he said okay, and we headed over to the 24-hour Casse-Croûte.

The wind was whipping up a storm over the river. We went by Mike's workshop. It was late and there was a night light on inside. I thought of poor Nuliaq, hidden under the workbench, alone on his old pillow, the wind shaking the sheet-metal roofing and making an ominous sound that he could surely hear inside.

"The roof needs fixing," said Mike every time a squall blew in from the open water.

He might have been hyper attentive to mechanics, taking exceptional care of anything that could be called a "machine," but he couldn't care less about his building. It was in a pitiful state. Last winter, when roofs were collapsing all over Quebec, my father had to convince him to shovel his roof.

I jumped down from the pickup and told Louis to wait for me a minute. The icy autumn wind hit me like a body check. Through the door, I could hear old Nuliaq in watchdog mode, beginning to bark. But as soon as she caught my scent, she quieted down, softly moaning. Through the window I could see her tail wagging. Something caught my eye: it was the old skidoo that Michel had found in Ontario, mounted on saw-horses. With its new bright green paint job you couldn't recognize it; the retro look was amazing. I could imagine Michel perched on the edge of his brand new, shiny leather seat waiting for the first snows of December to get into the woods and carve out kilometres of powdery trails.

The gate to the commercial dock was locked. Through the wind-swept drizzle, the red fog light blinked on and off every five seconds.

My father parked the truck on the west side of the dock, next to the boat ramp I used to get down to the water at low tide. We ate, listening to country music on community radio. In the distance, huge waves slammed into the pier sending plumes of spray high into the air, carried by the wind. It was warm in the truck; we were cozy.

After gulping down our hotdogs we turned up our collars, put on our gloves and went out. As the sleet lashed our faces, my father let out a few choice words. Then we headed down to walk along the shore. The tracks in the sand from my last quad outing were still there.

Now the dock and its bright security lights were far behind us, and we were in complete darkness, watching the frothing sea stirred by the storm. The fog light at the end of the dock ceaselessly blinked its warning, and I told myself that no sailor, no matter how skilled, would want to be out in this wind. They tell a lot of shipwreck stories around here that date back to when sailboats plied the river. Down at the docks old timers will tell you about a wreck lying in this or that place. And boats still run aground on the sandbanks that start out near Pointe-Noire and extend two miles into the sea. Even today, the St. Lawrence can fool the biggest cargo ships, no matter how sophisticated their technology is.

Standing beside me, my father told me about a boat that, in 1987, had been forced to cast off from the dock during a storm. It drifted onto the shale reef further offshore, its big diesels unable to overcome the combination of strong current, the rising tide and the north wind that was blowing that night. The hull broke apart on the sharp rocks. The sailors had all been rescued, safe and sound but the boat stayed out there for awhile. People came from all around just to see it, like a freak of nature dropped into the middle of the sea and mountain landscape. It only took two winters for the river to tear the steel hull to pieces and carry it out into the deeps.

Hands stuck in my pockets and tuque pulled down over my ears, I listened to my father's story, my gaze lost in the river's dark, magnificent and infinite mass.

The wind and the sound of the waves steadily rose over his voice and it became harder and harder to hear him. Suddenly, he took off running. He often does that when we walk along the shore, as if he can't help himself.

Usually, I run after him. But this time, I stood and watched him bounding like a wild broad-shouldered animal, his long hair flapping in the wind. He disappeared into the night, as though carried by the mist.

I bent down and touched the water's edge to sample with my lips the cold, salty water on my fingers, never taking my eyes off the sea, seeing Jessie's face in the wind lashed spume above the waves.

I don't know for how long I stood like that, a prisoner of my imagination. When I came back to reality, I saw my father coming toward me. The fierce wind drove the freezing rain parallel to the horizon. By now the tide was all the way in. It was impossible to get to the boat ramp. We had to take the long way and scale the fence at the municipal garage to return to the road.

By the time we got back to the pickup, we were drenched to the bone and chilled to the marrow.

⦿

The next day, the moment I set foot in the cafeteria, people crowded around to congratulate me and to shake my hand. In spite of my resistance, they dragged me to the table where my teammates and friends were sitting, Félix, Samuel and Tommy. We could do no wrong. Everyone was talking and joking around.

Despite all the brouhaha, I was silent, simply nodding my head at everything anybody said, but my mind was totally elsewhere, as if I was an astronaut in my spacesuit surrounded by beings from another planet. My eyes, ever alert, were hungry for a glimpse of Jessie. Three times I pretended to have to go to the bathroom; once to not pee, and twice to drink some water. But each time, it was really so that I could check out the student cafeteria.

I didn't see her. There was only Sauvé's gang and the other rappers, metal freaks, punks and miscellaneous groups, slouched down in chairs, sofas and colour cubes. Not once did I see her or even catch whiff of her. In fact, it was me who was being watched from the back of the cafeteria: her brother Stéphane had his dark eyes constantly locked on me.

All through the day, at break and at lunch, I roamed the school looking for Jessie. I never once saw her. And it seemed like wherever I went Stéphane Pinchault was staring at me.

Later in the day, after phys ed, I was sitting by myself at my locker, putting on my shoes. I sensed somebody's presence. Lifting my head, I saw Stéphane at the end of the row of lockers. I could see his face from the side, his head turned towards me. I froze, bent over, steadying myself on one leg. I smiled at him and waved stupidly, but he stiffened without a word. From where I was, I could see every last detail of his cartoon-like red nose, and the great big hairs that passed for a moustache.

Exasperated by his behaviour, I took a step towards him. He backed up, and then took off. I ran to the end of the lockers and looked down the hallway in both directions: one that led to the gym and the other to the administration and the cafeteria. He had completely disappeared, evaporated more like. Troubled, I ran up the stairs to my right four at a time; I was late for math.

After the last period, Tommy and I left school together. He wanted to go to the restaurant to hook up with the girls—again—and I asked him when he was going to help me get the cabin ready for winter; there was wood to haul and a hole in the roof to repair. He shrugged his shoulders saying he didn't know. We walked in front of the bus, through the crowd of students fighting like wild men for the best seats. There he was, staring at me again.

I lowered my eyes and pretended to be completely absorbed in the discussion I was having with Tommy, having something to do with handlebars that were overheating and burning the palms of his hands. But I couldn't pull it off. I just had to do something. Wait for me, I told Tommy and went up to Stéphane Pinchault, who didn't run away this time. He calmly held his ground and I waited for him to speak.

But he wasn't going to say anything ; it would be up to me to break the ice.

"What's happening?" I said.

He didn't answer. A little smile slowly crept over his thin wet lips, but something about his expression bothered me. I felt like I was about to lose patience and blow up, but I kept my cool. Because more than anything, even more than why he was acting so weirdly, there was one question I wanted the answer to.

"Is your sister around?"

Again, he seemed not to hear me. Except that now his smile twisted into a hideous grimace. I backed up a couple of steps, ready to flee. He raised his hand to stop me, and bent towards me. I listened as hard as I could. And he whispered, real low, as if he was afraid of being overheard:

"I figured out the secret code in the book. I accept the covenant. I'm ready."

I didn't have a clue what he was talking about. Not a guess. I shook my head from side to side in distress, raising my two hands to signify that I couldn't do anything to help him.

Hurry it up, the driver barked and Stéphane climbed in and took a seat. I watched as the bus pulled away, standing with one hand on my head, tugging at my hair.

"How's it going?" said Tommy, who had come up to me.

"He's nuts."

"If you ask me it's you who's starting to lose it."

◉

For once I said "yes." I went along with Tommy to hang out with his girls at the restaurant. Not that I really wanted to. It's just that I was completely bamboozled; Plan B for getting closer to Jessie had taken a bizarre twist. I was feeling sick to my stomach, and because of that I didn't really want to be all alone.

At Chez Lisette, we met up with his girlfriend, Karine, and her friend Chloé. We took a booth. Everyone ordered poutine or pogos, except me. I didn't order anything. Through the neon "OPEN" sign that flashed blue and pink in the window, I saw two truckers talking. One of them, pot-bellied and hiding behind a big moustache, pointed at his forty-five footer covered with snow. He had to make it to Sept-Îles. It was snowing up there. Soon it would be our turn to taste the first storm of the year. Already.

I wondered what they were talking about, the two truckers. They were probably talking about the weather. But also the road, what they had seen en route. Such and such village on the Côte-Nord, or in Tadoussac or Natashquan. I wouldn't mind driving a truck and seeing the country. I'd roll west all the way to Vancouver, or south to the United States. If hockey doesn't work out, maybe I'll be a trucker. And go far, far away from here, and stay away for a long, long time.

"Don't you want anything?" asked Chloé.

I lifted my heavy eyes toward Karine's friend.

I looked at her dark-skinned, round face, her long black hair. This girl was always smiling, as if her life was nothing but eternal happiness. She would crinkle up her almond eyes and begin laughing at any old thing you said. And to tell the truth, that was bugging me, so I wasn't very nice.

"No, I'm not hungry. Anyways, I gotta go."

"It was nice to see you," she replied.

She laughed and I ignored it, pretty sure that she didn't give a damn about me. I know I wasn't that "nice" to look at, what with the mood I was in.

"How come you don't want to stay?" asked tall Karine.

"Leave him alone," said Tommy, shrugging his shoulders and taking a bite of his pogo dipped in mustard.

When I got home, Sylvie told me that my father had headed out to the bush and wouldn't be back until next week. Apparently he had insisted that I go get the quad since a storm was in the offing. I ate in silence, and then went to my room to do my homework. Later that night I went to lay down with Sylvie in her bed. She was reading another one of those big novels that she tore through in a couple of nights, lying in her pyjamas, under the duvet. She doesn't do anything else at night. Do you ever wonder if everybody ends up like that when they grow up: alone, rolled up in their blankets.

I woke up the next morning in Sylvie's bed. It was warm and cozy, and it smelled nice, like her. I found her, dead to the world, asleep in my room. There were comic books all over the floor. Tiptoeing so as not to wake her, I gathered my clothes and left the house without eating. I was going to be late for practice.

It was early morning and still dark out. The days were getting shorter and shorter and the sun didn't rise before 7 a.m. The streetlights on the 138 still shone on the slick black pavement. A lot of snow had fallen during the night; the trees were laden with heavy wet snow, trunks bowed under the weight. Long clouds that looked like giant wisps of smoke moved across the dark blue sky over the river.

I took the trail that went down to the arena. But at the top of Fir Hill I stopped dead in my tracks when I realized that I'd forgotten my hockey gear. I don't know what had come over me. For a moment I considered going back to get my stuff, but there was no use, I couldn't get there on time anyway. I could just picture Larry beside himself, telling me that in the NHL I'd be suspended, fined, you name it.

Cars were pulling up at the entrance to the arena. At the head of the line, Samuel lifted his hockey bag out of the trunk of his parents' burgundy car, and then kissed his mother goodbye. Next came Félix and then the Bégin brothers. Last up, Larry hurtled in with his big Jeep TJ, proudly laying down some fresh tracks in the parking lot. He jumped out, clad in a leather jacket that I hadn't seen him wear before, sporting his tinted glasses even in the middle of winter with what was left of his hair flapping in the wind.

I stayed out of sight, leaning against a tree, watching them file in. I decided to take the Mill Road up to the Company Road.

My quad was flying at top speed through the snow and mud. Gas to the max, I passed the black spruce that lined the roadside like a guard of honour, but this time for a dark prince. I just about lost it on a couple of hairpins on the twisty road. I was too deep in thought to see the enormous ditch that had been cut by a backhoe at the intersection of 3rd Side Road. The Suzuki went in front first and came out the other side five feet in the air. I held my breath, ready for the curtain to fall. The landing was brutal. The suspension crunched when it hit the ground, as I did against the gas tank. The wind was completely knocked out of me. Bent in two, I tumbled to the rocky snow-covered ground. The clouds in the grey sky spun around my head like a whirlpool descending over my face.

I was out for a while, then came to slowly. My coat was soaked from the snow that had started to melt under my body. I could barely stand up. I just made it to the pumping station; parked right beside it was a yellow school bus.

The engine was idling, exhaust coming out the tailpipe. In front, the driver was reading a newspaper and drinking a cup of coffee, killing a few minutes before he started his morning route picking up kids and taking them to school.

Soon enough he slipped the bus into gear and started forward. I got back on the quad and followed him at a distance. When he stopped in front of the Pinchaults' dilapidated house, at first I stayed on the road, then drove down into the ditch so I wouldn't be seen. Standing on the seat surrounded by dried cattails, my snow-covered head shrunk down inside my big brown shirt, I saw Stéphane with a dark blue tuque on his head, running awkwardly to the bus. Not a sign of Jessie.

When I tried to get up out of the ditch, the quad had completely stuck in the mud. With one knee on the seat, I tried to free it. The tires spun in the muck and mud flew in every direction. A couple of times I fell into the creek, one time head first. It took me a good fifteen minutes to get out and not without considerable effort.

Finally free, I looked over at the Pinchaults' house. Obviously, gunning the engine like that had raised a racket and attracted some attention. I saw old man Pinchault and Jessie in their bathrobes on the old house's crooked porch. When she recognized me, she slammed the door and went inside while Robert Pinchault, a cup of coffee in his hand, watched me motor past his house down 3rd Side Road towards the school.

Not super cool.

The principal didn't like my reason for being late. I told him the truth: that I had been run over by a crazy trucker. How grungy I was should have been convincing. But he seemed to have his doubts since he said he'd be phoning my parents. I told him that wasn't necessary, but he insisted. So I gave him my special treatment for making people uncomfortable.

"My mom's not alive."

He sighed and apologized. He said he'd be speaking to my father and my aunt.

Since my clothes were filthy and wet, I spent the day in my gym clothes, keeping close to Tommy and following him around like a puppy. I hoped I wasn't starting to get on his nerves. He seemed constantly annoyed at me. I didn't know if it was because I had skipped practice, been rude to his friends or was dressed like an idiot. I would have rather kept to myself and not spoken to anyone, but I just couldn't. I always had this feeling that someone was looking at me, even when there were people all around me. No matter what I did to get away from him, he always found me. Stéphane Pinchault was beginning to scare me—seriously.

"How come you weren't at practice?" asked Félix at lunch, while wondering how he could get in with Karine's girlfriends.

"I went in the ditch. Larry must have been out of his mind."

"No. He didn't make a peep."

Instead, it was Sylvie who lost it. Apparently, the principal had told her that a truck had come close to finishing me off on the 138. I must be a crazy airhead, she said. My father was going to go nuts.

Acting like someone who has stared death in the eye without blinking, I happily gave her the details of what had never quite happened. The truck had gone off the pavement and come so close to me that I had to accelerate to escape. Unable to regain control in time, I went in the ditch. There was one little problem with my story: if anybody went up to where I said the accident had happened, they wouldn't find so much as a skid. Actually, the image of the truck made a big impression on Sylvie who began dissing the reckless drivers and trucking companies that worked the Côte-Nord. And then, like a perfect example of the nonsense that had been going on every day for a while, she said:

"Laurent called. He wanted to know why you weren't at practice. I told him what happened."

By now my own lies were closing in on me; I decided to park the quad for the winter. I fired a couple of pucks at the garage while I ran the engine outside, circulating fuel cleaner to clear the injectors. It started snowing again. After cleaning, greasing and lubricating the Suzuki, it was 7 o'clock when I finally covered it with a big green tarp and wished it a happy hibernation. My quad was like a bear that goes to sleep with the first snow. Come springtime, it would be famished and I promised it we would both feast on a ton of trails, that we'd go all the way up to the reservoir as soon as the snow melted to catch us some twenty-pound pikes.

The next day at school I saw Jessie.

I'd promised myself, after everything that had happened, to forget about her and get on with my life. My father had humiliated hers, there were the multiple indecisive trips past her house, her brother Stéphane was obsessed with me; in short, everything was massively broken and was never going to be fixed. My heart was messing up my life, big time. I had to focus on hockey. I had to rebuild my bridges with Tommy. And I had to start hanging out with his gang of girls before Félix got in tight with them.

All the great promises I had made to myself evaporated in thin air the moment I found myself standing in front of her.

Once a week, we spend an hour at the municipal library, which is connected both to the school and the community centre. I was walking through the shelves in the natural sciences section, looking for something on natural catastrophes. I felt like reading about tornados, tidal waves and volcanoes. But my eye was drawn to a history of boats from the first dugout canoes to the super tankers of today, from Roman galleys to Spanish galleons. There were amazing cross-sections of vessels. For the first time, I understood how the Vikings travelled in their long ships. The book claimed they were the first whites to come to the Côte-Nord. They must have been out of their minds to cross the Atlantic in their cockleshells of boats.

I looked up, and she was right in front of me. She seemed surprised, probably not expecting to see me there. She glanced from left to right, but she didn't leave. No doubt about it; it was an omen. I had so wanted to see her, and everything seemed to conspire to keep her away. This was my chance. So, I said hello. And she said hi back.

She kept looking down at the ground. Her eyes, so beautiful to me, were slightly veiled behind her long, curly hair. You could barely see her pink Pumas under her floor-length jeans.

"I want to say I'm sorry," I said.

"What for?" she said.

"My father…"

She shrugged her shoulders, brushing aside her hair with one hand so I could see her eyes, and looked straight into mine.

"My father hasn't drunk a drop since then. It's probably all for the best."

Suddenly I felt like I had wings.

"Thanks for covering for him."

"Thank the moose," I said.

"You wouldn't be the moose by any chance, would you?"

She winked at me and smiled. I'd have liked it to last forever. But she turned and I watched her disappear behind the stacks. I almost went after her, but I told myself that what had happened was just right, that it was just the beginning of something and that I had to be patient.

I thought about her all day. When a teacher asked me a question, I looked up, completely lost. Not only did I not know the answer, I didn't even know what class I was in.

At the end of the day I was leaving school when I saw her french-kissing Jon Sauvé, leaning up against his Honda.

Chapter Five

We were scheduled to take the bus to Sept-Îles the next day. As we'd be playing back-to-back games on Thursday and Friday Larry cancelled our last practice. I got there a little early. Usually, we're the last to show up, since Sylvie's always short of time. Once she even drove me in her bathrobe. Embarrassing.

But not this time. When I got home around two o'clock—we get out of school early on game days—she was waiting, ready to go. We were so early that we got to the arena parking lot at four, half an hour before the bus left.

Snow had been falling for an hour; the old yellow bus was covered in a fine layer of powder. Larry's jeep was parked next to the bus.

"What are you doing?" asked my aunt, clutching the steering wheel, the old wipers squeaking and creaking every time they cleared the windshield.

"I'm waiting."

"Waiting for what? There's the bus, get going."

"Waiting for the other guys. We're early."

"I know we're early. I'm sorry, but I've got a meeting."

"A meeting? What kind of meeting?"

"None of your business."

"Ho ho ho," I said, teasingly. "A secret little meeting."

"Get out, you big brat."

And she literally kicked me out of the car with her feet, with me laughing the whole time. I teased her some more while I was getting my duffel bag out of the trunk. Without another glance in my direction, she took off, leaving me standing there. Her hand waving through the open window was her only good-bye.

I went over to the bus. The driver pushed the lever, opening the door. As I got in, I looked over at Larry's jeep. It was covered with snow except for the still-warm hood where the snow had melted. You could clearly see the head of the lynx he had painted on it.

Up the steps I went, nodding to the driver, a new guy I had never seen before. As usual, Larry had taken the front seat. He was slouched down, his little reading glances perched on the tip of his nose, looking over his notes. He barely looked up as I passed. Uncomfortable, I went and sat in the last row. You could hear a pin drop. The snow was falling harder and harder. The guys started to file in, one by one. The bus pulled out, and even though the other guys were nervous with the upcoming game against Sept-Îles—a real good team—on their minds, I slept like a baby.

There I sat in the locker room, legs outstretched, just about to lace up my skates. Larry was talking about the game plan. I listened with one ear, not digesting much of it. With my quad garaged for the winter, I absolutely had to find a skidoo to take Jessie up to the cabin. I would sweep the ice so we could skate together. We would race (I'd let her win) and, when we got to the other side, there'd be a snow bank we'd both tumble into, one on top of the other, in the January cold under the stars. I came back to earth, surrounded by my teammates as we left the locker room under Larry's martial encouragement. My skates still weren't laced and I missed half the warm-ups.

As soon as the puck was dropped Sept-Îles pinned us in our own zone, coming hard on the forecheck. I tried to intercept their lead man but he got by me and ripped a bullet at our goalie who made a nice save with his pads. Gagnon grabbed the rebound, passed to Vigneault who relayed it to me at centre ice, where I was circling. *Break-away!* I was in alone.

But I did one dipsy-doodle too many trying to dazzle the crowd. The puck rolled away from me and I lost my balance trying to get it back. I slid into the back of the net, carrying the goalie with me. He was a big guy from the lower Côte-Nord, and he smacked me three or four times in the back of my head with his glove, mashing my nose into the ice to make me pay for taking his net off the moorings. I went back to the bench as a new line came on the ice. I hadn't even sat my bum down before Sept-Îles had scored the first goal of the night.

We were behind 2-0 at the start of the second. Larry double shifted me on the first and third lines, hoping to get something going. My legs were holding up okay. It's just that there was something missing … a fraction of a second. Usually I'm a step ahead of the play. I mean, I like to anticipate what the other guy is going to do and be the first one on the puck. That way, I can set up the play and whoever comes up to meet me has to hang back a bit. No one can beat me when I get to the puck at full speed. But as the game went on, I found myself reaching the puck at exactly the same time as my opponent and having to fight it out. I wasn't used to being on the receiving end of so many hard shoulder checks.

The physical play forced me to rush my game and I made more than my usual number of turnovers. At the end of the second period, we were behind 4-0. One of Sept-Îles' goals was the result of a glaring error—mine: a blind pass right onto the enemy's stick. In no time he was in front of the net and you can imagine the rest.

With two minutes left to play, we were down 5-0. Sept-Îles set up the trap, bottling us up in the neutral zone. It was over. But they kept hitting me anyway, banging me around. I was sucking wind, my legs were on fire. I tried to thread the needle between two defencemen with a crazy move that came more from desperation than anything else. They sent me flying. I landed on my back and smashed into the boards in front of my own bench. My teammates winced, as if they could feel my pain. Above them, wearing his tinted blue glasses, Larry was leaning over looking at me, his face expressionless, his arms folded.

◉

It was dead silent in the locker room. Larry started marking up our mistakes on the white board. That went on for a good half-hour. Me and the guys, all sweaty in our gear, watched him use his markers to diagram our ineffectual power play, our anemic back check, our deficient neutral zone game, our blown transitions, etc. At the end, the hockey-rink shaped board was covered with red, black, blue and green scribbles.

When he finally looked up and saw us, he realized we were whacked; nothing he'd said had gotten through. Sadistically, as though he took a perverse pleasure in torturing us, he said we'd cover it all again, tomorrow, before the next game.

"How's the ankle, McKenzie?" he asked.

I raised my head, surprised that he'd spoken to me. Coach stared at me, waiting for an answer. I could feel the weight of my teammates' hopes. They were waiting for an answer themselves—not some scribbles on Larry's whiteboard, but an answer that could only come from me, the team's star player, who only last season had led the team to the regional championships scoring twenty-six goals in the playoffs, a feat that had been written up all over the province and even made the Montreal papers. As if driven by an unconscious pressure, even though I hadn't really felt any pain during the game and even though I knew that it wasn't in any way the cause of my pathetic performance, I said that my ankle wasn't one hundred percent.

"Okay, so you sit tomorrow," said Larry. "We need you in top shape for the rest of the season."

I nodded my head as if that was the wise thing to do. My teammates were also nodding, looking at each other, as if that explained why we had lost and that as soon as I was completely healed, the team would be back in the winning column.

◉

The next day, it was another rabid crowd, this time at Baie-Comeau. I watched as we took a 7-2 licking. Félix was everywhere on the ice. The problem: he was the only one on the team. I really like Tommy—he's my friend—but he's just too slow. Samuel is fast, but he doesn't handle the puck very well. Vigneault, on defence, is another good player. He's big and he's an excellent skater, very mobile. There's nothing too much to say about the other guys. Unless you're talking about Bastien, in net, who does a good job with his long legs. The guy is skinny and not that strong, which is why it takes him a few ticks to get back up on his skates. But it's something to see when he extends the pads and does the splits to stop a breakaway.

In spite of the back-to-back losses, I woke up Saturday morning in a great mood. Giant snowflakes were floating to the ground. More than a foot of snow was on the way, said the forecast. I was sure that winter was here for good and we wouldn't be seeing the mercury climb back up over zero until the end of March, except for a few warm days sometime in February—maybe. Warmer days aren't always such a good thing in winter. They usually mean freezing rain and treacherous roads. A hard, frozen crust forms on top of the snow and it's bad news for skidoos. On the other hand, it's good news for lake skating rinks. Water pools on the ice and levels it perfectly, smooth as a mirror, forming a better surface than you'll find in any arena.

On the way home from Friday's game, the atmosphere in the bus was pretty heavy. I sat next to the window on the right side and watched the black spruce rolling by along the 138. There was a frozen pond, nice and round. I sat up on the seat divider to talk to Tommy, who was sitting behind me.

He was playing poker with Samuel and Dominic, a defenceman.

"Are you in?" he asked me.

"No. Hey, when was it we made the rink up at the lake, three years ago?" I asked.

"No idea."

"It got real cold real early, just like now, and we were skating before Christmas. It feels like it'll be like that this year too. What do you think?"

"I don't know," he said, not even looking up. "You let us know when it's time to do it."

I nodded and sat back down. It was finally sinking in, watching Tommy bluff and take the hand with a pair of threes: this winter, there wasn't going to be any rink up at the lake.

Someone tapped me on the shoulder. It was Sam.

"I didn't forget what you asked me about the other day, and I talked it over with my pa. He said my uncle François has one for sale."

"What is it?"

"A Yamaha."

"What model?"

"I think it's a Yamaha Bravo 250."

"Bravo?"

"Yeah, Bravo."

"Well, okay, bravo!"

"Listen, he'll give you a good price, around three hundred bucks."

"Cool!"

"The only thing is, it's up at Colombier. As soon as there's enough snow, we can go up there together. We'll make it a real good ride."

That's why I woke up in such a good mood. I laid out my skidoo suit, my gloves and big snow boots, and I tossed some eggs in the skillet and threw in some bacon. Sylvie came down in her pyjamas, her glasses crooked, perched on the tip of her nose, still half asleep. Her long black curly hair hung down on each side of her face in total confusion. She was barefoot on the icy floor.

"Mmm," she said, coming up behind me. "Tell me, champ, you wouldn't be making me some too, would you?"

"With broken yolks?"

"That's not very tempting."

"That's what I know how to make, eggs with broken yolks."

"You just need a little training. Make it two eggs over easy for me, yolks unbroken."

She sat down in her chair and put her feet up, rubbing them briskly to warm them up.

"What's going on, anyway? This floor's freezing cold. You have to get down to the basement and check the fuses."

"I don't know anything about that."

"Louis'll be back on Monday and until then, you're the man of the house. It's your job; go check it out. And before you do that, go get my slippers in the living room. It's too cold on my feet. I'm not walking on that freezing linoleum."

I put two over-easy eggs, yolks broken, and some bacon and burnt toast on her plate. She looked at her breakfast and frowned.

Then she said, "No coffee? You didn't make my coffee?"

"Hey," I said. "Are you some kind of princess all of a sudden?"

"Yessir," she said, "I'm a beautiful and magnificent princess."

"Well, okay."

I went to the living room to get her slippers. Sylvie obviously had found a boyfriend. When she sleeps in and stays in her pj's all day, it means she's dreaming in Technicolour. Now, what I had to do, and this was important, was to find out who it was. And if it wasn't Mike, I was going to have to put the screws to this relationship with any devious means at my disposal.

"So who is it?" I asked, standing in the Ceiling Fans and Lights department of Canadian Tire.

"What do you mean, who?"

She walked through Tools and disappeared down an aisle. But I followed behind and quickly caught up to her, putting on a good move and sliding with extreme agility between two shopping carts being pushed by two old ladies who were chattering away.

"You know damn well who I'm talking about."

"No I don't," she said, holding a hammer in her hand.

"You don't just suddenly become a princess while everybody's asleep, Sylvie McKenzie."

She put back the hammer and headed for Household Cleaners. She was going to have to do better than cleaning products; I wasn't going to let her skip away that easily. Little by little, she began to give ground.

"You don't know him."

"I don't believe that. I know everybody," I said.

"He's not from here," she said.

"No way. Everybody's from here. If it's somebody from out of town, I'd be on it as soon as he set foot in town."

She fled into Christmas Decorations. That did it. Christmas tree balls, garlands and innumerable idiotic multi-coloured plastic trinkets—I just couldn't. Especially when she began clapping her hands to get the little Santas bopping around singing "Jingle Bells." I had to get out as fast as I could. I reached safety in the Hunting and Fishing department, where I checked out a couple of bamboo poles. Sweet. Next year, I'm gonna get me a primo fly rod and go after some salmon.

At the checkout, she paid for a box of fuses with Canadian Tire dollars. I had figured out which fuse ran the two electric radiators; it was blown. Down in the damp, dirt-floor basement there was the pump, some outdoor furniture like the table and chairs for the porch, and shelves where Sylvie stored the tons of preserves she made. And you'd better watch out for mousetraps. I already got a toe trapped in one. Not funny.

It was still snowing. A big tractor sent snow flying as he ploughed between the parked cars. Sylvie, who had just sat down in the driver's seat, opened her window.

"What are you up to?

"I'm going to Mike's."

"Why?"

"Because."

"Stop being a pest."

"I'm not, I'm going to Mike's."

"Not a word to Mike, OK?"

"About what?"

"About nothing!"

I'm not going to write what she really said, because it's not her style to carry on like that. Let's just say she sent me rudely packing, which made me laugh; her reaction told the whole story. She left the parking lot spinning her wheels in the snow and I began walking towards the port, and then up to Michel's garage. I had forgotten to put on my boots, and in no time my shoes and cuffs were soaked.

Walking down the big hill that led to the port, I saw skidoo tracks going up and down the road. And I heard a two-stroke engine start up backfiring and then humming like a razor. Mike shot out of his yard like a rocket, his Maple Leafs hat on his head. He was riding his old green snowmobile, the Skiroule 440. He rode to the end of the dock and then pulled a U-ey and floored it. He must have seen me since he came right up to me. That's when the engine went perfectly silent, and then stopped.

Michel got down and walked with long strides some ways away, then came back, gesturing furiously, fake kicking his machine. He swore again when I caught up with him, hands in my pockets, nonchalant.

"Hey, Mike! What's up?"

He looked at me, exasperated. He was really furious.

"What's going on?" I asked.

"I don't get it, don't get it, just don't get it…. not a thing!"

He went on ranting while he stomped the heels of his cowboy boots into the snow.

Mike gives it one hundred percent. He's the best mechanic you'd ever want to know. And one reason for that is he's super patient and never loses his cool. The state his Skiroule 440 had put him wasn't normal.

I can't tell you what an incredible job he's done on that antique. Restored each and every part to the Wickham manufacturer's original specs. Not only was the paint job, leather upholstery and all the cosmetic finishing impeccable—just like new—but he'd rebuilt the entire engine, carburetor, transmission too. He attacked the work with the same skill and passion as the guy who had originally built this amazing machine at the end of the sixties and who, with the help of his family, manufactured them for over fifteen years until the company was bought out by Coleman from the States.

"It starts right up, every time," said Michel. "It runs for five, ten minutes, then it stops and it won't budge after that. Search me why!"

"Gas line?"

"No way!"

"There must be something there."

"Look, I've rebuilt everything, everything's new, it gets gas fine, the carburetor's perfect. Everything's rebuilt, everything! It can't not work. It's black magic, do you understand me?"

It had belonged to an old Indian from Ontario. He'd put a spell on it. There was no other explanation.

Would he give up? No chance. In spite of the thousand-year shamanic science that had cast an evil spell on that snowmobile, Michel was going to fix it, even if it took an entire lifetime.

We pushed it into his garage, and lifted it up with two hydraulic jacks. Mike became absorbed with his tools and his tinkering while I silently watched him open the hood and take apart the carburetor. I looked at Nuliaq, who hadn't even got up when we came in; lying on his dirty old red pillow, under the workbench, it seemed as though she didn't even know we were there.

"Is that the air intake, under the handlebars?" I asked.

"Yeah," he said, without a pause in his work. "When I was your age, I had an old skidoo that was just the same. We were ripping down 3rd Side Road at full speed. Just before the little hill at the tracks, where you wrecked with good old Pinchault, we dumped in some ether. We took off like a friggin' rocket."

He started laughing his head off, imitating the sound of a rocket, miming with his hands a spaceship. He lifted his cap and dried his eyes. I don't remember seeing that guy ever laugh so hard.

"Wicked."

"Yeah. I only did that three times. The last time, the head blew under the pressure."

"What did you do?"

"What do you think? I replaced it."

And he went back to work while I squatted down close to the workbench, extending my hand to old Nuliaq, who sniffed it and then licked me. Her grey and black fur was all ratty and she smelled bad.

It was Michel who caught me by surprise, even though I had come exactly for that reason. And I stood up and turned around, just like a kid who had gotten caught. He never lifted his head out of the skidoo's engine.

"How's Sylvie?"

"I don't know."

"She's got a new boyfriend?"

"Ah… I didn't know that."

"I saw her last night with some guy coming out of the movies in Baie-Comeau."

I pretended not to know anything about it. No need to mention that my aunt was all excited and that she had got her hair done, got all made up before going out. He'd seen her and he already knew about it. He'd been hanging with her for a lot of years. That's when I realized why he was so angry, not to mention his machine not working.

For him, fixing machines was sort of like trout fishing I figured. If his Skiroule didn't work, maybe it was because he was bothered and the engine sensed it. But I was pretty sure he didn't want to hear anything like that.

"I know why it doesn't work, the skidoo."

"Why?" he asked.

"It's your Maple Leafs hat... If you were wearing a Habs hat, no problem."

He threw a roll of electric tape at my head.

●

The next day, Sunday, it took me over an hour on the phone to bug Samuel into wanting to go get the Yamaha at Colombier. The snow really wasn't deep enough, his father wasn't keen, he didn't know if the oil had been changed, etc. He trotted out every excuse in the book and I shot them down one after the other saying that thirty centimetres had fallen just since yesterday and that I'd change the oil myself.

The last excuse was that he was afraid of the cold, that he was worried he'd get sick and miss tomorrow night's game. Of course, that was just the sort of excuse I was waiting for. After calling him a little wuss, a first-grader, etc., a couple of hours later we were flying along on his father's Bombardier Tundra, ripping along the Mani-couagan trail through the forest at top speed. It was dangerous. A couple of times we came close to cracking up. In fact, I fell off the skidoo twice, but didn't get hurt. On purpose, Sam whipped the skidoo back and forth like a maniac and I went tumbling through the snow right up to the trees. It was great.

After a demented trip of two hours we reached Colombier. Samuel quieted down once we got there. His uncle Normand, who had a huge potbelly and a big grey moustache, seemed surprised to see us. He went out with us to the garage in T-shirt and slippers, in the snow.

He had to strain to slide the big wooden door on its rail.

"Skidoo season starts early this year, boys," he yelled while starting the skidoo.

He drove it around the yard, and then across the field to the tree line. Then I took a turn. Kneeling on the seat, I banked left and right to test the suspension and the steering. After a couple of sprints, I got off, satisfied. It was missing some punch, but it'd be perfect for the winter. (Better than walking up to the cabin.) I took out the three hundred dollars I'd robbed from my piggy bank and handed it to Normand.

"How're the trails, boys?" he asked us while counting the money.

"Perfect," I said. "It snowed a ton up in the mountains. It's pretty deep."

And I indicated the height of my hips with my hand.

Samuel was tongue-tied and beat a hasty retreat, hoping his uncle wouldn't see the damage we'd done to his dad's Tundra. Fact was, there wasn't enough snow on the trail and we had smacked into a big rock near Betsiamites River. The right ski was all bent. His uncle wanted to pursue the discussion, but I revved the engine so hard that we couldn't hear a word he said. Sam jumped up on the Tundra and we were out of there like a couple of bandits, taking the upper trail fast as we could.

Well, okay, it's a heavy 250. Comfy, but not too fast. Samuel was really pushing me on the way home. He seemed permanently irritated and I think he was pissed because I had insisted on this whole outing in the first place. But it wasn't me who'd been driving the damn machine. If he'd been watching where he was going, instead of trying to dump me, he wouldn't have hit that rock.

Finally, he gave a big wave of his hand to let me know he was out of time and had to make a beeline for home. He disappeared into a stand of spruce leaving me behind in a cloud of mud and snow. I didn't mind. I was happy to be alone rolling along on my new skidoo.

The snow had stopped for the first time in two days. The sky had lifted and a little bit of blue was poking through the cottony clouds. The cold started to get to me. I went up and down the big trail that wound endlessly through lakes and mountains, passing through some breathtaking scenery. For miles and miles, as far as the eye could see, there was nothing but lakes and trees. And once in a while, it could even make you dizzy. Like when you cross a bridge and realize there's nothing underneath you, and you feel pulled towards the void. Here, it's the endlessness of the forest that enchants you and tries to lure you in deeper. What might you find if you were to go a little bit further, just to the other side of this hill, or that mountain, or behind those two trees? And even further than that? I felt like just doing it, like taking an unmarked turn-off that led to nowhere.

I left these rambling thoughts behind me with the blue exhaust of the two-stroke. Uncle Normand must have mixed too much oil with the gas. I'd have to check it out. The engine was making a weird noise and changing speed without me giving it any gas. Maybe there was something loose in the clutch. It was a whistling, strident sound that hurt your ears but that would stop with a sudden clack. That was going to be a job for Mike.

I began to get a little bit worried. If the skidoo broke down, I'd have to walk and I wouldn't get home before midnight. What bothered me the most was the cold, which was getting more and more intense as the day came to an end.

But quickly, all my troubles seemed for naught when I spotted the giant tracks in the snow on the trail. I stopped to get off the skidoo and make sure. They were moose prints, all right. They pressed into the snow right down to the grass. I doubled back on the trail to see for how long I had been following the animal. Lost in thought, I must have been following it for a while, since I couldn't tell where they first started. Yet, he couldn't be far off, given the freshness of the tracks.

I climbed back on the old Yamaha and kept going, nice and easy, expecting to see the moose at every turn of the trail. Finally, on a long marked curve I saw him, walking straight ahead, wagging his rear end from side to side, his huge antlers sticking out on each side of his head, covered with fir branches and snow.

I slowly got closer to him. He didn't seem bothered by me, or by my skidoo, as though he owned the trail and was saying, "Look, my good man, this is my home." I followed behind my trail guide for a couple of long minutes until my clutch did its noisy thing and, this time, the moose bounded off into the woods.

I jumped down to chase after him. But I didn't get very far. To my deep disappointment, the bush was too thick. The branches seemed to reach out and catch my coat, I had to give it up. My father, the great hunter, had often explained to me how a moose is able to move through the thickest brambles: he walks forward looking backwards. It's incredible that a creature that large can pass through spaces that you couldn't even squeeze through.

On the trunk of a large spruce, inside a long wedge in the bark, I found a tuft of the moose's hair. I knew it was him, again. This time I knew it; he was looking for me. I raised the tuft to my nose so I could catch his scent, then I got back on the trail, feet numbed by the cold.

By the time I got to the end of the Manicouagan trail, it was almost dark. I took the service road at the pumping station up to 3rd Side Road. Only one cross-country skier had come this way, and the recent snowfall was unblemished. It was like a racetrack and I remembered Michel's story about the ether in the engine and the jump at the railroad tracks.

I began to slow down when I saw the Pinchaults' house. I had made enough of a fool of myself already. I only had one thing in mind: to get past as quickly as possible and leave it behind me. There was light coming from the ground floor. The flickering white light of a television shone through the big front porch window. Suddenly, I noticed something strange and my hand stalled on the accelerator. A light was flashing on the second floor, maybe from a flashlight. It went on and then off with a pause of five seconds, then back on, like the fog light at the end of the dock.

I hesitated for a second. Then, unable to resist, I jumped down and crossed the Pinchaults' big field to the left of the house, with its mangy stand of pine, junk scattered everywhere, auto bodies, appliances, couches, mattresses and box springs, you name it.

Without losing sight of the blinking light, I approached the house, as though hypnotized, following the luminous signal that repeated with clockwork precision. I was within a few feet of the house when it stopped. I completely froze, like in a dream, when you realize that you don't know how you got where you are.

The sky had cleared, leaving a practically full moon that made the fresh snow sparkle. It lit up the house surrealistically, highlighting the large flakes of white paint peeling off of the grey clapboard siding.

The front door opened and I hid behind a withered old pine and a beat-up mouldy couch. Footsteps echoed on the old porch, which creaked as if it would collapse. For a moment there was a silence that is hard to describe, kind of like after a big snowfall, when the wind drops to stillness and the mercury heads south.

Nervously, I fiddled with the wet and frozen foam spilling out of a torn pillow. Then I saw someone moving on the porch. I recognized Stéphane Pinchault from his spindly silhouette and his legs that were too long for his body. He was decked out in a black leather jacket, jeans and white running shoes that gleamed in the glare of the moon. He pulled out his flashlight and pointed it at me. I watched him, through the springs of the old sofa, sending out one long flash every five seconds. I held my breath as though deep-sea diving and came out from where I was hiding.

He continued to signal me with his flashlight and as I headed towards the house, I stiffened my spine. I could hear Pinchault breathing, just a couple of metres away on the porch.

"What do you want from me?" I finally asked him.

He didn't respond right away. To my big surprise, he lit a cigarette with a click of a big Zippo. He took a long puff and slowly exhaled. The smoke hovered in the frozen air. No one said a word until the smoke had completely dissipated.

"I was waiting for you," he said, taking another drag.

"What's that about? 'You' were waiting for me?"

"Every night, for about a month, I've been sending a coded message out towards the forest. I couldn't see you. But I knew you were there, waiting for the right time. Tonight, the moon is full, and you've come. Now we can…"

"The moon's not full," I hissed, annoyed. "It won't be full for two more days."

He didn't answer, as if it didn't matter. And, it didn't actually matter. Everything seemed like it was about to shift into an alternate reality, an unreal dimension. My heart was pounding.

"Everything is all prepared up in the hayloft," he said.

"The hayloft?"

"In the old barn. Everything's ready for the investiture, the passage."

The front door creaked on its hinges and I scooted under the porch.

Through a gap made by a broken and rotted board, I saw it was Jessie. Her foot fell a few inches from my nose as she stepped over the gap without noticing me. Lying in the dirt, under the porch, in an uncomfortable position, I saw her come up to her brother.

"What are you doing?" she asked.

"Nothing."

"You're sneaking a smoke."

"So what?" he answered. "What are you sneaking?"

Jessie took out a flask hidden under her arm and brought it to her lips. She took a big swig and then exhaled loudly, as though blowing off steam. Her voice was raspy.

"Who were you talking to?"

"No one."

"You remember, Stéphane, what the doctor said…"

She didn't finish her sentence. From where I lay, I couldn't see what she was looking at. But I did see something come over her face, her expression changing from idle curiosity to indescribable horror. With a scream that curdled my blood, she scampered as far away as the porch would allow. I couldn't see either of them anymore. Jessie swore like a truck driver, using every possible swear word one after the other.

"That's totally gross! When are you going to stop doing that? Eh? When?!!"

She ran in the house, slamming the door behind her.

Since I wasn't about to hang around for the explanation, I was already out from under the porch and heading for the exits. Stéphane Pinchault jumped down on the snow behind me. He was coming towards me, walking slowly like the creatures in *The Night of the Living Dead*.

His eyes were shining like some kind of freak. I kept running through the trees and the junk, dizzy, not knowing which direction to take. I turned around just in time to see him suddenly materialize from behind a tree, right in front of me, speaking frantically.

"When are we doing it?" he said. "When? I need to know."

I wanted to tell him to go home, to go to sleep, that for sure he had some pills he should take. His tortured face was livid. His eyes were demented. He lifted his arm and held out his hand, red with blood. He was holding a dead rabbit.

Terrified, I ran for my life as he moaned behind me. I jumped on my Yamaha and I saw him, among the trees and the junk, twirling and shaking the rabbit in his outstretched hand. The snowmobile started right up and the clutch began whistling, squealing at the moon, the sound mixing with Stéphane's morbid howls. The lights in the house were all on. And, while Robert Pinchault and Jessie came out on the porch, I powered out onto the road that went by the house.

The Yamaha was moving at a good clip. With my teeth clenched, I squeezed the gas all the way. I couldn't get my mind off the bloody hand holding the carcass. My kind-of-broken headlight swung back and forth shining this way and that on the snow in front of me. I got to the railroad tracks and hit the hill going almost seventy-five kilometres an hour.

The skidoo thundered into the sky, losing all contact with the ground. I saw the town ahead of me in the distance start to shrink as though it was about to be swallowed up by the earth, and the black river overflow. I thought I was going to fly far out to sea and land in the ocean. Then the skidoo nosed down and I smacked the ground, hard. The snowmobile stayed on the road, but the suspension couldn't handle the impact and the two skis splayed out on either side, like duck's feet.

I made it home rolling down the shoulder of the 138, the left ski bent completely sideways and dragging on the asphalt, sparks flying. When I got to my driveway, I saw that I was leaking gas. Guess I was lucky I didn't set myself on fire.

Chapter Six

There it was, parked in front of the house: the big red pick-up. My father was home after a week in the bush marking trees for cutting. I'd planned to spend the evening wiping up the gas that had leaked out and cleaning the mud off the skidoo. Crouched down, I stared in discouragement for a long time at the two bent skis and the suspension that seemed to be shot on both sides. How high into the air had I flown?

I didn't have a red cent to spend on repairs. The gas line was leaking ... and who knows what else was wrong?

Then the garage door swung open. My father was standing in the entrance, plaid shirt half unbuttoned. His untied hair hung down over his shoulders. It was clear he hadn't washed up since he got home. He'd put on his big felt boots without bothering to tie them and the laces were dragging on the floor. I could tell from his dark face and his shrouded eyes he'd been drinking. Hands in his pockets he shuffled over to the Yamaha.

I'd gone up to Colombier with Sam, I told him. I'd gotten it for a good price and I couldn't wait until he got home from the bush because Sam's uncle Normand wanted to get rid of it right away.

"Good deal," he said, nudging one of the mangled skis with his foot.

I'd cracked up on the Manicouagan trail, I explained.

He started talking about my hockey future. If I didn't get serious or if I hurt myself seriously I'd miss the season and could probably kiss my dream of playing in the NHL goodbye. But he kept it short, ending with a sigh when he saw I was only half listening.

He added that Larry had called him.

Everything that had happened to me since I hurt my ankle seemed to weigh on him. It hurt him to see me less and less interested in hockey.

We discussed the racket from the clutch. I got the shivers just talking about it.

"Take it to Mike and have him check it all out. And tell him to change the suspension. It's on me. You did real good to grab it, the Yamaha. We'll need it this winter. But let's try to take care of it, okay?" he said, with a knowing wink of his eye.

"Okay."

He ruffled my hair affectionately, then headed for the door. But before he got there, he stopped and stood still for a long moment, as though petrified.

"How'd it go up at the reservoir?" I asked.

"They're closing the plant. They broadcast it on the evening news. It's over, working in the bush. I'm out of a job."

Then he stepped through the door and disappeared into the darkness. I could hear his heavy footsteps in the cold snow, then he climbed up the front stairs and closed the door. The fluorescent light flickered over my head.

That night I didn't sleep a wink. I tossed and turned under my blankets, haunted by Stéphane Pinchault's tormented face. The next night, at Baie-Comeau, we lost again, 5-1. I was sucking wind the whole game, just couldn't catch my breath. My legs were on fire. In the third period, Larry, exasperated, left me to stew on the bench. I couldn't find my rhythm. I didn't understand why. And in the locker room, later, the whole team was feeling hopeless.

◉

"So?" I said, leaning over Mike, who was working lying on his back.

"No, no, the only thing wrong is the leaky gas line."

"Great."

I had taken my Yamaha to Mike's the day after we lost to Forestville. He didn't have time to look at it right away, he told me; come back on Sunday. When I got there, I saw that he had rebuilt the suspension good as new and had even applied vinyl tape to make some orange and yellow lightning bolts to cover the scratches. I really wanted it to be in perfect shape, so I asked him to check one more time that it wasn't still leaking. Which he did, no questions asked. Because obviously I didn't know anything, and he was the top mechanic around.

It had been a strange week. We lost to Baie-Comeau, Saguenay and then Rimouski on Friday. Larry, fed up, assigned us exercises to do on our own at home. He told us he was going up to get his shack ready for ice fishing and that while he was spending the weekend doing that he'd be trying to clear his mind. He didn't want to see us before the next game.

And Christmas was only two weeks away.

That Monday morning, on the way down the stairs to get a chair for one of my classes, I bumped into her going the other way, books in her arms. She wouldn't look at me. I tried not to push it, reasoning that I'd already made enough of a mess of things. When I was just about to turn the corner at the foot of the stairs, I heard her ask in an exasperated voice:

"What's this?"

I stopped dead. There she stood at the top of the stairs, not moving, books pressed tight against her chest. Through the porthole-shaped window that overlooked the landing the cool winter light made her look even paler than usual. I went back up the stairs slowly, one step at a time.

There were dark circles around her eyes, which flitted here and there without coming to rest on any one thing. She recoiled a couple of steps, which made me feel horrible. I couldn't stand to think she was afraid of me. Which was perfectly understandable considering the way

I'd been acting for the last couple of weeks. All I had been hoping for was to see that enigmatic smile again, the one that had captivated me the first night I saw her ... But now the light in her eyes seemed to have gone out.

"What do you want?"

She said it in one long breath, as though she had just put something down that was too heavy to carry. Nothing, was what I wanted to say. Just to hold your hand.

Then, off the top of my head, I blurted out, "Would you like to go for a walk down by the shore?"

She seemed just as astonished as I was at the thought of it. Her mouth relaxed as a smile crept over her lips.

"Down to the water ... in winter?"

"It's beautiful," I said.

"You ... you know I'm going out with Jon?"

"Yeah, I know."

She smiled. Her tiny eyes had gotten back a bit of their shine and she shook her head from side to side.

"You're cute," she said, bent forward and kissed me on the cheek.

Then, she disappeared.

Her lips were warm and very soft. They'd barely grazed my cheek. I brought my forearm to my nose hoping she'd liked my smell. Hers was delicious. Not the smell of perfume, but the lingering memory of her long curly hair that had tickled the sides of my face when she'd leaned in close. All of a sudden, the light shining through the window had dimmed and she'd completely enveloped me, her face up against mine.

There I stood, in the middle of the staircase, one hand on the banister, playing over and over in my head that little kiss that had only lasted a second but that was still occupying all the space around me. Everything else had vanished. Then I leaped down the stairs as though I could fly and headed for the supply room on the run to get the chair.

◉

"Hope I'm not bothering you," said a voice, yanking me out of my daydream.

Michel was talking to me as he wiped his hands on an old greasy rag.

"Wha'd you say?"

"Are you even listening to me?"

No, I hadn't heard him. While he was doing a final check of the Yamaha, I had been off in another galaxy. My thoughts were making my head spin. Mike threw me a worried look.

"Are you okay, man?"

"Yeah, not too bad."

"Tough going, eh? The hockey, I mean."

"I haven't been the same since I got hurt. I'm not sure what's going on."

"Don't let it get to you. You'll get it going again. All the best go through at least one massive slump during their careers."

"A slump"… I nodded.

While we were rolling out the Yamaha with its orange and yellow lightning bolts and black paint, Mike told me he'd installed ten-inch skis since I wanted to ride up to the cabin and, with all this crazy snow, that's what you ought to have. He had completely taken the clutch apart and reassembled it. The motor sputtered to life with a cloud of blue smoke, and then began to purr contentedly. I was immensely relieved that I wouldn't have to hear that scary whistling that made me think of Stéphane Pinchault screaming his head off.

I was just about to start up the big hill when I noticed that Mike was standing there right beside me, hands in his pockets. He was wearing his light-weight motocross jacket that wasn't any good for this kind of weather. And of course that damn Maple Leafs cap on his head.

"Something you wanted to ask me?" I said.

"I took her to the vet," he said with a sad smile. "They don't give her long to live. My dog, that is."

"I'm sorry, Michel."

"That's life … I just wanted to ask if I could bury her on your land up at Lake Matamek?"

I held out my hand; he gave it a firm shake. I hadn't said anything, but of course the answer was "yes." He understood. I started up, swinging the snowmobile around in a half circle. The gate to the pier was open and I passed the security guard's shack; he didn't even look up. I pulled up to the fog light at the end of the dock. It was blinking on and off, on and off, like Stéphane's flashlight.

Off in the distance, there was a boat sailing up river towards Quebec City or Montreal. I imagined I was a sailor standing on the bridge. The icy wind would be enough to freeze you solid. Soon the ice would begin to form huge mosaics stretching from land out over the water. Then would come tiny icebergs shaped by the tide sticking their heads above water..

I looked out over the cold black water. On the other side was the Gaspé Peninsula. You can see the Chic-Chocs, looming up like giants, white with snow. They seem to be floating above the water and drifting like ice floes. If I closed my eyes and lowered my head, I could see them sinking, down down into the deep.

◉

I buzzed into our front yard at top speed, proud of my Yamaha that looked as good as new. The exhaust was still a bit blue, but Michel said he thought we should just mix more oil with the gas. I wasn't going to argue with "the artist." When I could afford it, I'd buy me a brand new four stroke … but for now, I'd have to make do with what I had. Waiting, with a big smile on my face, I gunned the motor sending up a big cloud of exhaust. I was hoping to see my father come out on the porch. But then I noticed that the big red pick-up was missing. Parked in its place, next to Sylvie's Toyota, was a black BMW.

I tried to remember how long it had been since anybody had come over. My father and my aunt would visit some distant cousins at Christmastime, but that was about it. A couple of Sylvie's friends would drop by for a drink the odd time, but I was pretty sure none of them were driving around in a BMW. In fact, I was as sure as I could be it was Sylvie's new "friend."

Now I was kicking myself. Why did I make all that racket gunning my skidoo when I pulled up in a cloud of snow. If I'd only known I had a chance to catch them in the act, I would have kept it down. No way they hadn't heard me. I hadn't even closed the garage door behind me when I spotted a man in his forties leave the house. He was tall and blond, with a black trench coat and the latest in shoes. He closed the door and walked down the stairs, gripping the banister so he wouldn't slip.

He walked through the snow-filled yard lifting his feet high to keep the snow out of his cuffs. He waved at me and flashed a Colgate smile, sort of like a politician on the campaign trail. Then, rolling slowly in front of me in his black BMW he waved once more and ran his hand through his long blond hair, then blasted down the 138 like a bank robber making his getaway.

I understood what Michel must have felt when he saw Sylvie with this guy. I didn't know what to think, but I knew it stunk. At the same time I felt very happy. If he had just been a friendly face, that would have made my life a little more difficult. But this, this was going to be too easy. This fish was big, slow and swimming in shallow water. A big old carp, the kind you can catch with your bare hands and kill with the whack of a stick.

Standing in the living room, I took off my coat and boots. There was a shadow moving around in the kitchen. The fridge door opened, and then the shadow poured itself a glass of pop. I called out in a soft voice.

"Sylvie, are you there?"

"What is it?" she answered, her voice irritated.

I heard her putting the bottle back in the fridge and I hurried to block her path to the stairs. I got there just in time and she ploughed into my chest.

She looked at me, steaming, and I smiled back.

"Let me by," she said.

"Who's the dude?"

"Alex, cut it out. I'm not in the mood."

"Come on, just tell me his name."

"It's Gordon, okay? Now leave me alone."

"What? Gordon!"

I was so stunned that my fish was named Gordon that she eased right past me and dashed for her room. I couldn't believe that the guy I had seen outside with the blond hair and the wing-tips was named Gordon. This was going to be so easy. He was already sizzling in the pan. Taking the stairs four at a time, I slid my foot in the door just before she could slam it.

She let out an angry yell. I had definitely pushed a button. That felt good.

"Gordon!" I repeated.

"Yes, Gordon. It's a name like anybody else's. No worse than, say … Mike."

Now, that was something that I seriously disagreed with. I pushed open the door and entered the room, lecturing her and shaking my index finger at her.

"No, no, no," I said. "Mike, that's a cool name. Michel, Mike, that's perfectly acceptable, okay? *Golden Gordon…* No. Sorry. That just doesn't cut it."

"Chr… You're an idiot."

Frustrated, she yanked the sheets off her bed and shook them at me before gathering them in her arms. I caught a disagreeable whiff. Lowering my arm I looked at my aunt, eyes wide-open.

"Sylvie! Your sheets stink. They smell like … yuck! They smell of *Golden Gordon*!"

I fell to the floor pretending I was choking, both hands around my throat, mouth wide open, eyes rolled upwards. She stepped over me and fled with her sheets, but not before giving me a kick in the stomach. I followed her, thumping down the upstairs hallway like I'd just inhaled poison gas. She locked herself in the bathroom, flushed the toilet, started up the washing machine and turned on her hair dryer, singing at the top of her voice to drown out whatever I was going to say.

I went downstairs to make some peanut butter on toast, feeling quite satisfied with my performance. It had been pretty convincing, I think.

The holidays were coming; you could feel it everywhere in town. There was more traffic. People were on their way to Sept-Îles or Baie-Comeau. Convoys formed up and people drove together to Quebec City, staying in a motel for the weekend and spending the whole day shopping in the big malls. You know, some people are really crazy about shopping, but there's others that live to party, I mean, really party. Seeing some guys crossing town honking and yelling, you'd think that they were already in New Year's party mode.

Thursday, it was standing room only in the arena. It had only been Tuesday that we'd actually beaten Rimouski. And Larry, who had been away working on his fishing cabin, came back in a great mood and had seen in that triumph—modest though it was, against the team that occupied the league basement, just below us—the sign of a rally. I'd scored a goal and made two assists. But the real hero was my centre, Félix, who'd skated like a wild man. I don't know if I was so hot as it seemed. It seemed to me that things were going better in spite of my presence, that I was operating on autopilot, but not much more than that. We'd have won and I'd have gotten my three points even if I'd been fast asleep.

Up high in the bleachers there was a bunch of guys wearing garlands around their necks, Santa Claus reindeer hats and Rudolf red noses. They were laughing and screaming their heads off. No one believed all they had in their soft drink bottles was Sprite. They were smashed out of their minds and they hadn't come to see their hockey team go down to defeat.

The first period went pretty well. My second shift, I took a beautiful pass from Samuel. In full flight, I let the puck roll between a Sept-Îles defenceman's legs and cut around him. The goalie came out to challenge me. I lowered my left shoulder, telegraphing my intention to cut to centre ice. He went for it. I went straight to the net and lifted the puck on my backhand.

The crowd applauded that goal for a long time. But they suddenly went dead silent, except for the bunch of drunken rowdies high up in the rafters who began squirting everybody with beer. The crowd heaved. People were yelling. And the security guard, poor Mr. Bégin, had his hands full. The referee stopped the game and both teams looked up towards the stands to watch the show.

The rest of the period we spent stuck in our own zone. Sept-Îles forechecked us relentlessly. Twice I was on the receiving end of wicked hits.

And the drunks, up high, screamed with pleasure every time I went down.

"Come on, McKenzie. Get up!"

During intermission, while Larry was diagramming his plan for the second period, I was in the first-aid room. I needed stitches on my upper lip, which had been jammed against my face-mask and split open when they'd driven me into the boards. I was creamed once again after that. The other team took a roughing penalty, but that didn't stop my ears from ringing.

In the second period, the game got even more physical. They continued to forecheck and our defence had its work cut out for them. At thirteen minutes, Gagnon spotted me at centre ice. He put a beauty right on my stick. Full out, I blew by two defencemen who had joined the attack and misread the play. I was in alone in front of the goalie who I easily beat five hole. Once again, the crowd went nuts. I raised my arms and my teammates skated over to me.

I felt a sense of relief. My legs were coming back. My wind was good. And my instincts seemed to be on the mend, along with my coordination. I was back in my groove. Everything was on its way back to normal.

Larry, all ramped up by the two-goal lead over the toughest team in the league, dished out orders left and right, marching up and down behind the bench. We had to trap, shut down the game, protect the lead and wait for an opening to attack.

We were lined up for the face off when we heard the crowd start screaming. I turned around just in time to see a dead rabbit, trailing blood as it slid along the ice. It came to a stop right between my skates.

My legs started to wobble. I didn't know what to think. Most of the fans were showing their disgust. Others started laughing, including the gang of drunks. An unspeakable rage came over me, and with a cry that could be heard from one corner of the rink to the other, I slapped the rabbit right back at them. It didn't even get close. The poor animal came apart in mid-air. Quite a few spectators were hit by pieces and splattered with blood. It was definitely sickening.

Everyone in the crowd was yelling at me. When I got to the bench, the expressions on the faces of my teammates were more than perplexed. I don't think anybody understood why I had done what I did. Larry, eyes popping out of his head, ran over to me and began yelling.

"What the hell is that all about? Are you nuts?!!!"

I headed for the locker room. At the end of the period, Sept-Îles scored its first goal of the game.

Between periods the mood was glum and then some. I stuck to myself, sitting in front of my locker, not speaking or looking at anyone. Larry, who had already forgotten the incident, still pumped up at the thought of a possible victory, had taken out his whiteboard and was frenetically drawing while emphasizing that we had to jam the neutral zone with all five players to bottle up the enemy.

And all I could see was that rabbit sliding up to me.

"McKenzie!" snapped Larry. "Are you listening?"

No, I wasn't listening. My ears were buzzing. I sat there, sweating in my gear, holding a bottle of Gatorade, with a feeling like none of this was real. I was sure I was losing it.

I came back on the ice for the third period with my head in a whirl, my mind completely muddled. I made bad decisions every time I was on the ice, contributing to four Sept-Îles goals in a span of twelve minutes. The crowd was incensed. No doubt cranked up by the rabbit event, they showered us with insults. Me especially.

Larry climbed up into the stands to fight the drunks. That night was pathetic.

As I left the locker room, the coach stopped me in the corridor.

"Practice tomorrow," he said.

"I'm not coming to practice anymore," I said, pushing past him and continuing on my way.

Sylvie was waiting for me in her little car. She barely looked at me during the ride home. She couldn't have believed her eyes when she saw me shoot a dead rabbit into the crowd.

The pick-up wasn't there when we got home.

"What's Papa up to?" I asked.

"He's spending some time out in the bush."

That night, in my room, I pulled down my posters of the 1993 Canadiens Stanley Cup team and my favourite player, Vincent Lecavalier. I stuffed them in the back of my closet and stretched out on my bed. Now the walls of my room were bare.

I told myself it was all for the best. There was nothing more to worry about. It was obvious; I'd have to quit school and find a job. Only, there weren't any more jobs around. Nothing said I couldn't go live in the city, anyway. I'd get my own apartment in Quebec City and study mechanics. I'd work with Mike. We'd build up the business and that would be cool.

The next day, I woke up with a killer headache. There was still a buzzing in my ears, it seemed like my mental confusion was going to last for a while.

I took off on my skidoo, no tuque, running shoes on my feet, hunting jacket unbuttoned. I must have looked like an idiot. I rode my Yamaha all day through the woods. It had rained all night. A thick fog had come in from the water, heavy with rain that began to fall, quickly changing to freezing rain. A thick coat of crystalline ice soon covered the forest. It was beautiful, but threatening in the way it seemed to crush everything that was living under its weight. In every direction, you could hear branches collapsing under the weight of the ice. The loud cracking played a gloomy symphony in the forest.

Up beyond my father's *natau-assi*, at one end of Lake Matamek, the trees that had been clear-cut by the Company stretched off into infinity like a cemetery, their stumps sticking up like tombstones. "Here lies a tree that once stood." What could the Company say now that it had closed its doors? Nothing. The city boys had scooped up all the money, and our men were poorer than ever. And what was going through my father's mind?

I went around the lake and came to the cabin. When I got there, I saw skidoo tracks in front. That didn't bother me. It's common knowledge that the cabin is available to anyone who wants to use it. The only rule is, tidy up before you leave.

There were footprints in the ice. I figured that someone had been there the previous night. When I opened the door, I felt like I had been punched in the stomach. From a cord that stretched from one side of the cabin's only room to the other hung seven rabbits strung up by their paws. They were dead and frozen. The blood drained out of my face. I jumped on my snowmobile and went zooming across the lake as fast as I could despite the dangerously thin ice. I took the Company road that led to the beaver dam.

It must have been about three o'clock, I can't really remember exactly. Robert Pinchault's car was gone and all the lights were out. I drove the skidoo up the unshovelled driveway and cut the engine in front of the porch. Stationary, I waited for what seemed like a long time; the only sound was the crack of falling branches.

A strange noise, like a rusty old pulley, drew my attention to the barn, at the back of the yard. Through the cracks between the old grey boards, I could see a glow. A trail wound from the side door of the house to the barn. I followed it, hands jammed in my pockets, feet freezing in my running shoes that were slipping on the ice.

The heavy door swung open, creaking painfully on its hinges. A disturbing smell struck my nostrils. I couldn't describe it, but it made me think of death. Then I spotted it, an old horse that could scarcely lift an eyelid when it saw me; I heard a couple of chickens clucking. A thick layer of dust covered piles of junk that must have belonged to Robert Pinchault's father .

The land had once been cultivated, but now it was littered with garbage. An old tractor with its tires removed was resting on woodblocks. One of them was cracked, so the poor machine was sinking into the ground. The entire barn sagged in the middle, as if the earth were slowly swallowing it.

Inside the barn, through the planks over head, I could make out a dancing light, flickering like candlelight. It must have been what Stéphane Pinchault had called the hayloft. On my left, some stairs led to the loft, where they must have kept animal fodder long ago.

I climbed slowly up what seemed more like a ladder than anything you'd call stairs, then pulled myself up into the loft where I came upon a number of dry old dusty hay bales. They had been piled up to form a wall with a small opening in the middle that functioned as a door that you could only get through in a squatting position.

Once through to the other side, I came upon something as hard to believe as it was horrifying: a couple of hutches piled one on top of the other full of live rabbits. And as if that wasn't enough, there were at least a dozen big vivariums, swarming with flies and insects of every kind, bred in vast quantities and heated by 60-watt bulbs. All you could hear was the incessant buzzing of the little bugs. With my nose right up against one of these revolting cages I could make out thousands of white maggots squirming and wiggling on a lump of furry flesh.

But the saddest thing of all was the line that stretched across the barn with dead rabbits hanging from it, a squirrel and a muskrat. And beneath this morbid scene was a table set with knives and some candles sitting in big puddles of dried yellow wax.

I picked at the dried melted wax with my fingers while staring at the bloody knives. A sudden sound startled me. All at once, my blood turned cold and shivers ran up and down my spine. Someone was coming up the stairs. There was no time to hide, a shadow had appeared in the little opening in the stacked hay bales.

Her hair was down, ratty, her face drawn. Her grey cotton pants were tucked in to fur-lined boots that were too big for her. In one shaking hand she held a bottle of bourbon. She came up to me with a twisted smile.

"Hey, champ. What do you think of little brother's work of art? Sick, eh?"

She laughed, uncomfortably. With a trembling hand, she brought the bottle to her lips and took a huge swig.

"What a cool house, eh? What cool kids Robert Pinchault has! A boozer and a nutcase."

She gestured at the grotesque scene. Then, nonchalantly, she stepped forward and offered me the bottle. I refused.

"I'd have thought," she said, "that once you'd of checked out this little house of horrors from top to bottom, you'd have been ready to call it a day and leave us the hell alone. What do you think?"

What I actually thought was that my life had been a nightmare ever since the day my quad broke down and I decided to get help up at the Pinchaults'.

After these harsh words, Jessie's face softened. Her big green eyes were opened wide, shining dimly.

"What did you expect? I've lived like this all my life. That's why I don't hang out with nice pretty boys like you. What I get are the jerks like Jonathan Sauvé."

And then she added, coming closer:

"You know, it's really cute, you using my brother to get hooked up with me. That's definitely getting you where you want to go and you know it, don't you."

She pressed up against me, her hands on my arms. Her breath was warm, but the boozy smell turned me off. She was smashed and I didn't want to encourage her, but she was insistent, planting her lips on mine. I tried to squirm away; no luck. I gave in without thinking what was right or wrong or anything else.

I squeezed her, holding her against my chest. I kissed her icy lips, drinking in her bad breath, her furred tongue coiling around my own. And there, suspended over our heads, like sprigs of lethal mistletoe, hung a row of dead animals.

She pushed me away just when I was about ready to go for it. Someone, or something, was moving in the room. We weren't alone. Someone was making disgusting noises with his mouth. Slowly, but surely, we could make out Stéphane Pinchault walking along one of the huge beams that supported the barn's roof. He was totally naked, shamelessly exposing his disfigured face. He was swinging an old rusted pulley that made a terrible squeaking noise in his hand.

Jessie snapped out of her stupor as if she'd stepped out of a cold shower, walked below the beam warning Stéphane to take it easy. He pretended not to hear her and kept swinging the squeaking pulley and making weird noises. Then, suddenly, he threw the pulley as hard as he could at one of the vivariums, which shattered in pieces. A cloud of insects swarmed out and filled the tiny room

Like someone who's seen a ghost, I dashed across the icy ground in my running shoes. I slipped and fell a couple of times, and snow packed into my sleeves. I jumped onto the Yamaha and took off. On the road, I passed Robert Pinchault on his way home.

I didn't sleep a wink that night. I was in bed at nine o'clock sharp, to Sylvie's astonishment. I tossed and turned under the covers, eyes wide open. My window was frosted over. There was a deep arctic chill outside.

Next morning, I stayed home from school; my life had changed and I should be preparing for my mechanic's course in Quebec City. I got on my skidoo to tell Mike the good news. I knew he'd be glad to hear that from now on we were going to be partners.

When I got to the shop, I was upset to find it empty. As far back as I could remember, Michel had always been there from morning 'til night. But not today. There wasn't any sign of him. Instead, there was a photo of Nuliaq duct taped to the window of the front door. I yelled out her name and kicked the door to wake the damned dog up. But I'd never hear her bark again. She'd never again lick the hand I held out to her.

The boat ramp was covered in snow. The tide had dumped a big pile of ice in the way, but someone had opened up a way through. I didn't have any problem getting down to the beach. A couple of seconds later I killed the engine. It shuddered once or twice and shut off.

Dawn was still breaking and the sun shone through the icy mist that rose off the water, filling the sky with pale pink light. Thick masses of mist, moving like clouds, would occasionally part to reveal a breathtaking vista on the distant shore and the Chic-Choc Mountains of the Gaspé. Only along the St. Lawrence could you see a landscape like that. Then it came to me. Once I'd met an old woman, a painter, who told me that she came here every day she could remember and never saw the sky the same way twice. It was always different: every day, every hour, every minute. That's one amazing thing about living close to nature. You realize how, like everything else in life, it's constantly changing; sometimes magnificent, sometimes horrible, but always alive.

A layer of ice had formed that extended thirty metres out from the beach. You could hear it cracking under your feet. Seated on my snowmobile, I turned and saw Jessie walking towards me, all wrapped up in a big blue wool coat. Her long curly hair rippled in the gentle breeze. She came close. Her thigh brushed against mine.

"Hi," I said, as if expecting to see her.

"Hey," she said, looking at the ocean. "Thanks for inviting me here. It's true that it's beautiful."

"I've been coming here since I was little."

"It takes your breath away," she said.

She stared deep into my eyes. I saw her freckled face and her mane of hair, where the sun had come to weave a delicate aura. Her eyes were creased. And she smiled constantly, as if her heart was filled with immense happiness.

She put her hand on my thigh, supporting herself as she leaned toward me.

Her hair barely touched my face. I found myself just inches from her now, and her breath, warm and sweet, with a hint of mint, caressed my mouth. We were in a spaceship, on another world, sheltered from the cold and the wind from the sea. Her lips met mine. Our tongues touched and we kissed, very softly, with a tender shyness. Warmth flooded into my stomach. I wanted to take her in my arms, but she held my arm to stop me. For a brief moment, her cheek brushed mine.

"I'm sorry for what happened yesterday," she said.

"I should be the one apologizing. It was my fault."

She smiled and gave me a final conniving look, eyes blazing.

And then, suddenly, without any warning, she started running full tilt towards the water. I watched, thunderstruck, as she ran across the ice only to disappear beneath the broken mirror of the sky. The ice sheet had cracked open, exposing patches of black, and she had vanished.

I started up the snowmobile. I gunned the motor three times and flew like an arrow towards the river. I slid for about twenty metres before the ice gave way under my weight. I had built up enough speed to surf on top of the water, as if headed towards the mountains, until inertia took over and I sank too, headed for the bottom.

The contact with the frozen water was a total shock. It blasted my senses, grabbing me by the arms and legs, kicking my survival instinct into full play. I frantically struggled with the thin pieces of ice that couldn't support my weight, finally touching the rocky bottom with my feet. My hunting jacket and snow pants were soaked through, but somehow I managed to climb onto the ice floe.

I crawled forward, chilled to the bone, with only one thought in mind: get back on solid ground. Someone was running towards me from the pier. It was Michel, screaming. My vision was blurred, I couldn't make out his face, as if there was a thick white fog between me and the rest of the world. The only thing I could recognize was his damn Toronto Maple Leafs hat. He looked so stupid with that hat. I couldn't understand what he was saying. I knew he was holding me and tearing off my frozen clothes. I was paralyzed, powerful tremors shook my heart. I was freezing to death. I closed my eyes.

Chapter Seven

There sat the Dark Prince in his armchair, watching the coloured lights blinking on the tree.

Christmas had been a total bust. My dad cashed his first welfare check and Sylvie found out that Gordon was married and had two kids. As for me, I was still recovering from the acute hypothermia that almost got me. I spent my days in the house, wrapped up in blankets, unable to venture outside.

Clearly, Jessie had not been on the beach that day. It was one monstrous hallucination, except for my plunge into the river at minus twenty. My Yamaha lay on the bottom, carried along by the shifting ice and the tidal currents. In my pocket was her letter asking me to forgive her, they'd sent her little brother to a psychiatric facility, she told me, and she had gone to live with her mother in Quebec City. She ended the brief but compelling letter by asking me to look out for her father.

When I was a baby, my mother left the house one day in the middle of winter, leaving me alone in my cradle. She walked down to the beach through the snow. Then she left her clothes on the beach, and walked out onto the ice floe until she disappeared. I never knew her. And I was twelve years old before my father could bring himself to tell me the truth. When Michel brought me home and told him what I'd done, he sat, grief-stricken, on the sofa for quite a while. He was reliving his worst nightmare: his son had re-enacted the greatest tragedy of his life.

Throughout my convalescence, at the hospital and then back home, Louis looked after me with tender care. He told me one story after another about the Nitassinan Innus and their amazing adventures, both spiritual and moral. I watched him immerse himself in the deepest reaches of his childhood, tapping into memories long since buried, and every day I sensed a little chunk of cold melt in my heart and the timid flame trying to re-ignite.

On the night before Christmas, we were all seated in the living room in our pyjamas around the Christmas tree, watching a holiday special on television with popular singers and movie stars. It couldn't have been more boring. But we were all down in the dumps; watching TV was the only way to get our minds off our troubles, thanks to all the glitz on the tube.

I gave my aunt some windshield wipers and my father a pair of mitts. Sylvie gave me some fishing flies and a sci-fi novel. From Louis, I got the bamboo pole I had lined up at Canadian Tire—I suspect my aunt had been watching me in the store that day—and a Montreal Canadiens baseball hat. I hadn't changed my mind about quitting hockey. My father hadn't said a word about it. Except that something in that gift expressed what he really hoped for down deep. I thanked him with a handshake, but I didn't put it on.

I dress warmly. Ever since my sad escapade, I'm pretty sensitive to the cold and I have to make sure I'm always wearing a warm tuque, a wool scarf and good mitts. Otherwise, for sure I'll start shivering and it'll be hours before I can stop.

At the beginning of January, a few days before school started, something was really bothering me. I had to face up to it. One morning, I got up early with the idea of going up to the cabin and back on foot. I'd be snowshoeing the trails for a good couple of hours.

It was the first time I'd been out since that fateful day and I was pleasantly surprised to find the temperature comfortable for that time of year. I crossed the 138 carrying my backpack, my snowshoes in my hands. I put them on in the ditch at the edge of the forest, using my poles to pull myself out of the ditch, and zigzagged briskly between the trees. I continued walking down Mill Road as far as the trail that led to the cabin. It took me almost two hours to get there.

Around the cabin, there were skidoo tracks and footprints. Somebody had been there. When I opened the door I saw that everything was in order. They'd restacked the woodpile with hardwood. Some branches on the floor filled the place with their piny scent. And to my great pleasure, the rabbits that Stéphane had hung on the cord had been removed.

I was anxious to shed some clothes and start the fire, but I just couldn't handle sitting down. My legs were twitchy and I felt like I could walk for hours. I shut the door behind me and walked up to my sitting rock. The sun was shining and the light reflecting off the frozen lake was brilliant. I sat down on a pile of snow and ate the sandwich Sylvie had made for me: venison, pickles and cream cheese. One of my favourites.

After relaxing for a few minutes while the sun warmed my face, I walked down to the lake, which was frozen solid. The wind had cleared the snow in a number of spots, uncovering the thick pale blue ice. It was rough and bumpy. I had to squint and shield my eyes from the sun in order to see the big bay and the beaver dam at the far end.

I walked to the dam with my snowshoes attached to my backpack, prodding the ice with my poles, as if to test its solidity at every step. After pausing for a moment to scan the horizon from the top of the old dam, I jumped down to explore the bog. There were plenty of animal tracks, including deep moose tracks I recognized right away.

I followed the tracks and saw a number of holes in the bog where the moose had dug up the grass that hadn't yet frozen, due to the heat produced by the layers of moss and organic material accumulated over time.

The tracks led up to a pile of old weather-beaten grey logs where I found the moose's antlers.

There were two giant pieces that could have only belonged to the unusual animal that had been stalking me since autumn. With the onset of winter, the male loses its antlers, which begin to grow again in the spring. I felt great sadness sweep over me, but great happiness, too. I came back to the cabin with a light heart and spent the rest of the day hanging up my trophy on the wall beside the stove. Before leaving, I also hung the Canadiens hat that Louis had given me, and then headed home.

The first week of school was pretty quiet. My teammates invited me more than once to sit with them. But I declined. Not because I didn't want to see them, but because I knew perfectly well that the only thing they'd be talking about was hockey. I didn't want to hear them talk about the games they'd played or the upcoming games.

Tommy came over and sat down across from me to find out what was going on.

"What the hell happened?"

"I don't know, I just flipped out. I wanted to test the ice, the engine got out of control and there I was, in the water."

We both laughed.

"So, what are you up to?"

"Not much, I'm going up to the cabin. If the ice is nice, maybe I'll do a little skating."

He simply smiled. Then, the bell rang and we went to class.

Friday night, I was ready to leave. The next day, I walked up to the cabin, with my skates in my backpack. I had peanut butter and bread for next day's breakfast, and a big piece of rabbit *tourtière* in a flat Tupperware.

I spent Saturday getting a good fire going and scraping the ice with an old aluminum scraper that I found under the cabin. Wearing my skates, I pushed back the snow to clear a big rectangle the size of a skating rink. Then, despite the bumpy and uncomfortable surface, I skated for close to an hour. The fresh air filled my lungs and I could feel the warm blood pumping through my veins. Feeling at peace, I watched the winter sun set behind the endless forest. I saw a plume of smoke rising into the pink and purple sky off in the distance, behind the mountain, over where the Company had logged the tall spruce. The sky was full of stars when I got back to the cabin. Inside, it was warm and cozy. I spent the rest of the night in front of the woodstove, in my boxers, warming up the *tourtière*.

I slept deeply, without dreaming, wrapped up in my sleeping bag on a carpet of pine branches. I woke up with a start. A two-stroke engine, the typical sound of a snowmobile, was coming closer. I was sure of it, hearing the way the sound, amplified by its own echo, reached me. As I was getting dressed, I heard it pass far off. Before I could put on my coat and lace my boots, the sound stopped. Then, after a couple of seconds, I heard someone start to swear. Unable to find my tuque, I grabbed my Canadiens hat hanging from the moose antlers and went outside.

Standing outside was a tall guy with long blond hair, a blue hat on his head and tight jeans stuffed inside his cowboy boots. He was yelling, obviously at the end of his rope, literally kicking a green snowmobile. It was a 1970 Skiroule 440.

Mike! And there on the lake, out in front of my cabin, he had met his Waterloo. He was actually taking his anger out on a machine; an unthinkable response he would surely regret at some point, considering his near maniacal kind of care, driven by excess love, for anything you could describe as mechanical.

"Hey, big Mike," I said, feeling in a real good mood as I ambled toward him.

Now he was cursing.

"That skidoo still messing with you?"

Still more curses, as he put the swear words together in brand new combinations of the juiciest French Quebec had to offer. I sat down on the dreaded skidoo. The leather seat felt comfortable. I squeezed the handles of the chrome handlebars. It was an awesome machine, for sure.

"There's some sort of curse on this thing," he said nervously.

"Uh …"

"I already told you, it's not human. It's possessed!"

"Come on, Mike. You know just as well as I do it's just a machine. There's a solution for every problem. You just overlooked some little detail. A tiny detail. If you think it through, you're gonna get it."

What I said made plenty of sense, but it didn't seem to get through to him. In fact, it wasn't even remotely likely to calm him down, considering he had rebuilt everything more than once, and considering that he was a great mechanic who had probably reached his mechanical wits' end more than once before now. I was tempted to say that he had taught all this to me, back when he gave me a hard time for not checking my plugs. But I quickly thought twice about it when I saw him turning red as a tomato, his eyes bulging out like he had lost it. For a moment I was worried he'd jump on me and wring my neck.

"Listen, smart ass," he said. "If you can get it running and drive it around for a while and it stays running, it's yours, okay?"

I turned away. I had one knee on the black leather seat and one foot on the ground for support. I cranked it once, strong and sure. The engine started up like a charm and began to purr contentedly. I sat my bum down on the leather seat and settled in. Then, pulling my Canadiens hat down over my ears I lit out like there was no tomorrow.

I went across the lake and back; the snowmobile showed not a sign of wanting to stall. Smiling the dumbest smile your could imagine, I made two or three circles around Michel, fishtailing on the ice. He watched me, incredulous, shaking his head from side to side. Then, in a rare display of elegance, he took off his Maple Leafs hat and tossed it at my feet. Happy now, I straightened out the Skiroule and gunned it, moving along at top speed, as if I could reach the sky.

By the time I got back, Michel was gone. He'd decided to walk back on my snowshoes. I don't know if you've ever seen someone snowshoeing with cowboy boots on? Me neither. It must have looked weird.

◉

I couldn't stop thinking about Jessie's letter asking me to look after her father. But I didn't even feel like going close to their place. And even less to see Robert Pinchault and talk to him. But now, cheered up by my new snowmobile, I decided to take my unlucky 3rd Side Road, just to check things out.

The big car was parked in front. But all the house lights were out, as if nobody really lived there. Out back, the old barn's roof sagged under the weight of the snow. I kept the engine running and sat there, motionless, wondering what to do.

When I saw the living room curtains move, I cleared out in a hurry.

I drove the Skiroule slowly along the railroad tracks. Then, since there was no way I was going to ride on the shoulder of the 138, I took the trail that went behind the arena. There, on top of Fir Hill, I saw the bus waiting for the team, on their way out of town for four days. They were scheduled to play four times in as many nights, including games in Lévis and Rimouski. I could see the burgundy van of Samuel's parents, who were giving him last-minute advice and reminding him to be sure and do his homework and not to eat too much junk food. The bus's engine began to rumble and then it circled the parking lot before climbing on to the highway, its windows caked with mud.

I coasted to a stop and parked the Skiroule in front of the house. Then, I cleaned it lovingly, trying to wipe up as much water and brush off as much snow as I could. The green paint gleamed under the neon light. I lowered my eyes when I saw her on the porch, a dish-towel thrown over her shoulder: Sylvie, with a question in her eyes.

"So, how'd you like the *tourtière*?"

"Scrumptious," I said. "Thanks."

"What are you doing on Mike's skidoo?"

"I solved a problem he couldn't. He didn't believe me. We made a bet, he lost, and now it's mine."

She frowned as if it was just another of my inventions for getting out of doing something. But this time my story was true.

I was in the kitchen washing my hands when I noticed that the pick-up wasn't there. When I asked Sylvie what was up with my father, she shrugged her shoulders. He had a contract in the bush; he was gone for awhile, she said. I didn't ask for any more details. That was all she knew.

There was one helluva storm that week. The electricity was out for three whole days, and we had to get our heat from the little stove in the basement. Sylvie and I played a lot of cards by candlelight.

She took frequent breaks, watching the snow fall and fall, blown by huge gusts of wind that shook the whole house. She was worried about my father. As for me, I spent hours looking out my bedroom window wondering where he was. Where could he be staying? What company was going to give him any contracts at this time of year?

School was closed. Getting around town by car was tough, but I had my green machine. On days like those, after a big winter storm, people would drive their snowmobiles right down the streets as though they owned them. They'd go to the grocery store, the pharmacy and the gas station. The town was full of the sound of loud engines making a wicked racket. And everybody would be in a good mood. They talk about the storm, they joke around and the next thing you know, the neighbours would be inviting you over for dinner.

I was in Mr. Simon's little hardware store to buy a box of six-inch nails and an axe that I wanted to bring up to the cabin. I overheard some guys shooting the breeze in the aisle next to me while I checked out the prices of a couple of tools. They were talking about the roof of Pinchault's barn; it had collapsed under the weight of the snow.

For a while now, I'd been keeping my head down, my Habs cap pulled tight over my ears. I know everyone recognizes me wherever I go. And I know they're all wondering why I quit hockey. They won't talk to me about it, but you could feel it. I barely waved to the old-timers standing around shooting the breeze, then I hopped onto my skidoo.

A big snow-plow on train wheels was clearing the tracks in the direction of 3rd Side Road. It cleared the rails with a big triangular shovel that pushed the snow to both sides. At the wheel, I recognized Jean St-Pierre with a cigar stub between his teeth. He flashed me a big thumbs-up when he saw the Skiroule.

What the two men had been talking about was true: Pinchault's old barn roof had collapsed. The structure on both sides was still standing. It was the middle section, weakened by age and weather, which had failed to support all the snow. Robert Pinchault emerged from the rubble and looked over at me. I felt like disappearing, but he waved to me. I hesitated, not sure what to do, feeling awkward. But, remembering Jessie's words so intensely it seemed like she was at that moment whispering in my ear, I got off the skidoo and walked over to him.

He wore a flat woollen cap and a plaid shirt similar to mine, in different shades of blue. A cigarette hung from his mouth, the smoke curling under his yellowed moustache. He looked at me with a little smile and with eyes that seemed clear, maybe for the first time. Pale green eyes, with Jessie's sparkle.

"How's it going, young man?"

"Pretty good. I'm sorry about what happened, Mr. Pinchault."

"Bah… It's no surprise," he said, hands in his pockets. "I should have seen it coming. I've got plenty of wood out back. I guess I just never had my heart in it."

On top of a pile of debris off to one side, I saw what was left of the rabbit hutches, with broken glass sticking out. Robert Pinchault had begun to clean up the mess. He'd even gathered up all the weird stuff his son had accumulated in the hayloft. The old horse, which had survived, was tied up behind the house. Only the tractor was still parked where it had been before.

He talked about his plans for the spring. How he hoped to rebuild the barn. His grandpa had built it and it was the least he could do to rebuild again before he died … Make things right on the land …

"Since I screwed up all the rest," he added with a long sigh that he exhaled with the smoke of his cigarette.

I cleared the snow off of my rink at the lake. It took me more than an hour. I kept turning to watch the smoke ascending from the cabin through the trees. There was an arctic chill in the air and the stove was so cold that I filled the cabin with smoke trying to get the fire started. I wanted to make sure it would burn heartily through the night; they were predicting minus thirty. For a moment, I watched the stars twinkling over my head, growing brighter as the sun sank. And for the second time, I saw a column of smoke rising up into the sky in the distance. I figured it would take me at least an hour to go there. I came back in to have a bite to eat without bothering to get undressed. As soon as I had wolfed down my dinner, I put on my skates and went out under a clear sky to skate under the stars.

I had my old Koho hockey stick and I practiced my stop-and-goes, moving laterally, making my abductor muscles work. I practiced until, exhausted and out of breath, I collapsed onto a snow bank to watch the magnificent sky, which began whirling around in circles.

All week long I went up to the lake after school to skate, getting home real late.

Sylvie complained that there wasn't anyone at home any more. And both of us began to seriously worry about my father; it had been quite some time since he'd contacted us. I spoke with Mike who hadn't heard from him either. Nobody I asked had a clue about where Louis McKenzie might be. When I mentioned the contract he was supposed to have gotten, the eyebrows went up around Mr. Simon's hardware store, everybody exchanging glances.

The following Saturday, there was someone on the lake. To be precise, I didn't actually see a person, but there was a fishing shack mounted on skis that someone had pulled out to the middle of the bay. Parked next to it was a snowmobile. Smoke was coming out of a black chimney pipe. It was the first time to my knowledge anybody had ever installed a shack this far from town. You see them all the time on the river estuaries, but on a lake like this, no.

I skated in the afternoon, but not for long, since a wicked wind was blowing and my feet quickly froze up. I only got off a few shots at the old net, held up by an ABS drain pipe. Louis had made it when I was eight. It was all crooked, and there were big globs of yellow glue hanging all over it. It wasn't regulation size, but I always thought it was pretty cool to shoot pucks at something more or less put together out of plumbing pipe.

That night, while I was warming my feet on the stove, I heard the sound of a motor. I went out, and standing on the little porch, I saw the light of a snowmobile moving along the middle of the big bay, near the dam, disappearing behind it. My fisherman was headed back to town on 3rd Side Road.

He came back the next day and the day after that. Then, he disappeared for a couple of days only to show up again the next week. When I realized that he hadn't moved the shack from where it was in the middle of the bay, I decided to find out once and for all who was fishing there.

I'd gone to the butcher's to buy some chunks of heart and liver. Then I walked out to the middle of the lake, a spot I knew real well, about two hundred metres from the mysterious fishing shack. There I bored a hole through the ice, made a snow bank in the shape of a half-circle to protect me from the wind and made myself at home. It only took a couple of minutes before a magnificent grey trout appeared, hooked to my line.

I stood up, fists high in the air, proudly watching it wriggling. As I had expected, the shack's door slammed open and shut. Some guy wearing a pale blue warm-up suit came up to me with a firm step. It was Larry.

By the time he reached my spot, I'd hooked another one, not quite so big this time.

"Hey, McKenzie!" he said.

"What's up, Larry?"

"What's the trick? I've been fishing two weeks up here and haven't caught a damn thing."

"That's because you're just too nervous, Larry."

He glared at me. He was freezing in his light-weight jogging togs and he shifted from one foot to the other. I certainly wasn't about to mention that down at the bottom of the bay, you couldn't catch a thing in winter. Except for right where I was, there was a depression where the current flowed, where the lake followed the curve of the mountain. The large trout hung out there grabbing food as it passed by. Not to mention there was more oxygen in that part of the lake and the fish could breathe better.

"Too nervous, eh?" he said.

"That's it, Larry. There's no doubt about it, the fish can sense you at the other end of the line. I'm not tweaking you. If you don't stay cool, they don't bite."

"Mmm, if you say so. Hey, McKenzie, you know what? I've been watching you working out up here for a while … Not too shabby, your skating."

And later that night, in a scene that could only be called surrealistic, I found myself running stop-and-goes under the stars with Larry yelling out encouragement each time I changed direction. His whistle echoed up and down Lake Matamek.

Next day, my mind was made up. I was going to take the Skiroule up the Company road as far as you could go. I put together a survival kit with food, blankets, matches, my axe and a jerry can of gas. At six in the morning, just as the sun was rising, I began the journey that was due to take me until after nightfall.

It was a beautiful day. There were a few fleecy clouds scattered over a dark blue sky. Black spruce lined both sides of the road while I put away the miles, one after the other. I crossed the Manicouagan trail and its snowmobile tracks, well-groomed by the hordes of snowmobilers who had passed by. Then, I continued travelling north, heading deeper and deeper into the dense forest.

I went through several clearcuts before stopping in front of a road that cut off to my right. Right at the cut off I could see a vehicle buried under the snow. I went to check it out. Noticing that a piece of red metal was sticking out, I started digging frantically thinking it was my father's pick-up. I tumbled forward trying to clear the snow off the driver's side door. When I saw that there was nobody inside, I relaxed. After a little more effort, I succeeded in opening it.

On the seat there was a pair of sunglasses, a couple of country music cassettes, a can of Pepsi on the floor and the wrapper from a garage sandwich. I looked for tracks, but there weren't any. No one had been here since the last snowfall, that was clear.

I saw a cutting zone down at the end of the side road. I put on my snowshoes and started out through the ravaged terrain, pushing on with difficulty through the stumps and debris: branches, brush and all the rest. Far in the distance, I could see the column of smoke I had already seen several times before from the lake.

Carrying my survival kit and my axe, I used the smoke, which climbed straight up to the sky, as a guide. It could only be seen under these exact conditions—with no trace of a breeze.

I lost sight of it as I came down into the hollow of a valley. But I'd noted carefully its location in relation to the countryside; I could tell I was getting closer. It took me nearly half an hour to reach it. I was once again in a cutting zone. I realized I was actually behind the mountain that overlooked Lake Matamek from the north. The cut came down the west flank right to where I stood. I was in my father's *natau-assi,* his ancestral hunting lands.

And, at the far end of this giant cemetery at the edge of the forest, where the Company had spared a stand of tall spruce, I saw a prospector's tent with a stove-pipe that gave off a thin stream of black smoke. I ran to the tent, driven by an exhilarating energy. Inside, I found a small four-legged camp bed, a table with some books whose pages were stained by soot and sap, and a stove made out of an old metal barrel. Behind the tent, there was a hut, crudely constructed out of branches and bark. As I opened the little door, held in place by a post wedged in at a forty-five degree angle, what I saw took my breath away.

On branches strung together with twine hung a string of hares. They'd been butchered; there was nothing left but the skins, with their beautiful winter coats. The meat was stored in a big metal box below the skins, carefully arranged in pieces of cotton cloth.

As I stepped out of the cabin I saw Louis McKenzie coming out of the woods carrying a huge beaver on his shoulder. He was wearing his high moccasins and his old sinew snowshoes. He had always teased me about my high-tech aluminum snowshoes. For him, there was nothing like moccasins for feeling the earth under the snow … and the silence most of all. When he saw me, a great big smile spread across his face. He showed me his catch with an indescribable sense of pride.

His long greasy hair hung heavily over his shoulders. The skin on his face, lashed by the wind and the cold, was red and looked thick as an animal's hide. Visibly fatigued by his load, but happy beyond measure, he tossed the beaver at my feet.

"Get a load of this! I've got another one in one of my traps. You have to come and get it with me. I've got some things to show you."

"Your camp is cool, Papa."

"Not bad, eh?"

We began walking towards a lake I had never seen before. That afternoon, I learned how to make an under-ice beaver snare. His father had taught him, and now I was hanging on my own dad's every word. Methodically he explained how you bait the trap with aspen branches and how you make the snare with brass wire. You slide it through a hole you make in the ice and secure it with a big branch that you put perpendicular to the opening. We scattered them all along the underwater path the beaver follows from his lodge to his food cache. The animal drowns under the ice, trapped by the loop that tightens around his foot or body. All you have to do is break the ice to gather your catch.

That night, we skinned the animals and cleaned the pelts, hanging them next to the rabbits. We ate the meat for dinner and we talked far into the night.

"After it storms, the trails became impassable by truck. I didn't want to be too far away if I was going to be checking my traps every day. I didn't catch a thing and I had to eat my bait. But then today, two in one day!"

"We were worried about you."

"I've been waiting for you for a while, son."

My smile grew wider and wider as I listened to him telling stories, by the light of his makeshift stove that had turned all red, fed by the burning embers. And honestly, I had to laugh when I found out that he'd been the one who had hung the rabbits up at my cabin, in December, hoping I would follow his tracks in the snow.

His cousin in Montreal promised he would pay a good price for the hides. He figured that would let him make it through the winter, and then he could enrol in a reforesting program and spend the summer replanting the *natau-assi*. He said he planned to get serious about working with Sylvie; he thought the gathering business could go pretty smoothly.

The next day, we tied the skins and the metal box to a sled that we made out of birch bark and lashing twine. We made our way back to town, driving slowly, my dad with his back to mine, keeping an eye on our treasure to make sure it stayed put. We stopped for a moment to climb up on top of the beaver dam and look at Lake Matamek.

There was smoke curling up from the chimney of the fishing shack and a skidoo parked to the side.

"Who's that?" asked my father.

"It's Larry, my coach."

"What's he doing fishing out on the bay? Did you tell him where the good spot is?"

"Yeah, yeah. I don't get it. He's got his own idea where to fish."

We turned down 3rd Side Road. Robert Pinchault's barn looked all straightened out. They'd removed the debris from the collapsed roof and piled them out of the way. The facing on each of the sides had been removed and scaffolding had been set up. Some brand new beams had been erected in a courageous attempt to rebuild the roof of that antique structure.

After telling Louis to turn around and hold on tight, I put the gas to the max and we took off at full speed.

◎

The Skiroule's engine seemed about to blow out. It turned at breakneck speed, the packed pistons detonating and screaming furiously at the forest and the mountain. My father suggested I cut the speed, but the sled with its load of furs held together. And, as we gathered speed towards the railroad tracks, I could feel him tight against me wrapping me up with his great big arms. He began to howl at the top of his voice like a madman:

"Ya ya ya!!!"

We hit the bump at the tracks at more than a hundred kilometres an hour. We immediately shot into the air like a helium balloon. We flew high, real high, the town below us lit by the streetlights that had come on in the early evening. We could see the river clearly—its massive blocks of ice sailing by—and the far-off mountains. We flew and flew, as though on a flying crazy carpet, over the 138 and a huge truck filled with logs, heading west. The fog light at the end of the dock noted our passing with its red and unruffled signal, reflected on the ice as far as we could see, every five seconds. We climbed even higher, as if we were clouds. We crossed the St. Lawrence and flew beyond the giant Chic-Chocs of the Gaspé.

◉

Larry paced up and down the locker-room, beside himself with excitement. He had come up with a system guaranteed to deliver a victory that night. The game had to be ours. This eternal optimist was never going to admit defeat as long as he still had one foot out of the grave. He waved his arms and rolled his shoulders, a marker between his teeth; a production that by the end reminded you more of a clown than a dictator. And from out of nowhere, he stopped talking about his perfect game theory and began to tell everyone about the incredible trout he'd caught the day before up at Lake Matamek.

There wasn't a soul in the room that wasn't skeptical. They turned towards me ... and I nodded in agreement. I had definitely seen Larry pull up that trout after having suggested that he move his shack.

Nobody seemed especially surprised to see me, suited up, sitting in front of locker number eight. I'd been put on the disabled list, and now I was back. You could cut the tension with a knife: our last-place team sensed it had a chance to win. That night, under the orders of sergeant-coach Larry, who threw out some mind-boggling shift changes to counter our opponent's lines, we won convincingly, 5-2.

The wins kept piling up and we clawed our way up the standings to steal a spot in the playoffs. Playing one of the most boring styles of hockey ever invented, we worked our asses off, all five falling back into the neutral zone and setting up the tightest trap you ever saw. We set about it with courage and determination, totally buying into the system. That forced the offence to pass the puck around until they made a mistake and then, ever on the lookout, I had a chance to intercept and take off on a breakaway.

The opposing teams' fans were furious. They howled at the moon like poor wounded puppies and hollered that we couldn't play the game and didn't even know how it was supposed to be played. But the only thing that mattered to us was to win. And we marked each and every victory with a big six-inch nail that we stuck into a fetish stick we had put right in the middle of the locker-room. We made it to the finals against Sept-Îles and swept the series in four games.

That year, in the playoffs, I collected nineteen goals and fifteen assists, finishing as top scorer.

In June, we all worked on Robert Pinchault's barn. There was myself, Samuel, Gagnon and Vigneault, Louis my father and Larry. We had just nailed the last shingle on the roof when everyone looked up to see Sylvie's

Toyota screeching into the driveway. She got out, running over to us, both arms in the air.

"Alex! They called. They called!"

I'd been invited to the training camp of Quebec City's major junior team.

I'd just turned sixteen.

See www.barakabooks.com for news about the second title in Sylvain Hotte's Break Away trilogy and about other great books.